IN THE ASHES

R.L. NELSON

For my brother and sister,
I don't know where I would be in life without you.
But it wouldn't be here.
I love you both

Contents

Dedication iii

1 Anywhere but Here 1

2 Medusa 16

3 Cosmic Love 35

4 Dead Man Walking 51

5 Dead on the Beach 71

6 In The Shadows 90

7 Big Bad Wolf 105

8 Whose Side Are You On 122

9 I Am Not A Woman; I'm a God. 131

10 In The Moonlight 139

11 Burn 154

12 The End 168

Two Years Later 174

Acknowledgements 176

About the Author 179

IN THE ASHES

1

Anywhere but Here

"Tonight, dual wildfires burn out of control in Arizona, consuming over twenty-five thousand acres and leaving a path of destruction. Gusting winds and dry condi–," The box TV shut off mid-sentence, the sound of static crinkling across the screen, leaving me to stare at my blurry reflection in the blank screen.

"You shouldn't be watching that." Zagreus tells me, he's sitting on the edge of the other bed in the motel room. This motel is really dated. The walls are yellowed, the flooring is that same patterned carpet you'd see in an arcade or a movie theater in the nineties, and of course the giant heavy box tv across from me has about an inch of dust on the top. The entire place smells like mildew and I'm not entirely sure what the stain on the floor in the middle of the two beds is.

In the corner, Andrew is sleeping under the table that he has turned into a blanket fort. Originally, he was going to sleep in a bed, but the curtains covering the window are paper thin and don't block out the sun enough for him. To be fair to him, the paper-thin curtains are why I was wide awake at sunrise this morning. But I am more than a little grateful to be getting my own bed. After traveling across three states and staying in our fair share of cheap motels, we've been sharing beds or sleeping in the car and Andrew has always been a kicker.

I start my way over to the dirt lined door of the motel room, "Where are you going?" Zagreus asks me.

I roll my eyes, "I need fresh air." I tell him as I leave the room, shutting the door with a loud *click*.

Outside, the motel isn't any better. Leaning into the rusty wrought iron fencing on the landing I take in the dull rocky landscaping with only a stained green swimming pool complimented by a broken diving board to bring any sign of life to this barren wasteland. All the buildings are the same sad beige color that most desert cities use to "match the landscape". Even the random placed cacti look thirsty.

The sun is still out, but in about an hour we'll wake Andrew, pack our things and head back out on the road again. Since Andrew became a vampire, our travel has been limited to the night. He can be in the sunlight, but only for a little bit because it drains him—whatever that means—and if we can't get out of the sunlight he has to be covered with a thick blanket. We even put an extra layer of tinting on the back windows of Zagreus's Jeep so he would be more comfortable.

I admittedly don't know much about Andrews' transformation. He hasn't been very talkative about his time in the underworld, and I didn't want to push him at first, but I find myself growing more and more curious about what happened to him. I've observed more about him than he has told me. Like how even though he drinks the blood Zagreus gives him, he doesn't ever seem to be full. It's like he's on the edge, not quite hungry enough to say anything, but not full enough that he turns it down. He also still has the same appetite for real food as he did before he turned, still needs—sometimes for way too long—the bathroom, still needs to sleep, basically he still acts and looks, exactly like a human, aside from the blood drinking. But at the same time, Andrew is also stronger and faster than before, his skin looks better, and his hearing is almost better than mine. There were a few times I found him almost entranced as he stared at someone, almost as if he could hear the blood pumping through their veins, and his instincts were telling him he needed to hunt.

That's the thing that scares me the most about him; that at any second, he could be an entirely different person. Almost like what happened to my little sister.

The night that Deme had her vision doesn't even feel real to me anymore. "*The end is coming.*" She'd said to us. Something in the tone of her voice didn't even sound like her and even after that, it was like she was possessed. A shell of herself.

Fear, violence, war, and death.

Zagreus went immediately into action. Calling my father and Nix back from hunting the Vry, even bringing Aphrodite back from Gabby's house, all while I held my sisters shaking body. I felt completely useless. I couldn't focus on anything but my sister. The way her eyes rolled into the back of her head, how she was shaking like she had been dunked into below freezing waters, how her voice sounded like three other people were speaking through her at the same time. Zagreus relayed everything to my father and the others, the exact phrasing, what he thought it meant. Aphrodite even agreed with him. We didn't know how, but Ares must have learned about something. Whether it was the Vrykolakas coming, Andrew turning, or my fight with Melinoë, we didn't know, and it didn't matter. Ares was about to wreak havoc on the world.

And it is all my fault.

It was Aphrodite that suggested we find as many allies as we could in hopes to fight back, Zagreus, agreeing with her for once, set the plan into motion. We left the next day at sunset and began our cross-country road trip, searching for Gods and not-so-mythical beings to join us in the war against Ares.

We weren't the only ones who left Paradise either. The remaining Vrykolakas disappeared without a trace, like they were never there in the first place. Only a few of the wolves stayed behind to keep an eye on things, the rest left, in fear of being hunted or used as a weapon. Instead of coming with us, Phoenix decided that his time was better spent searching the country for other packs of wolves, ones that might be willing to help us fight Ares if it came down to that. He had done some research and found that there could be another pack of wolves somewhere in Wisconsin.

Dad and Deme left paradise for a different reason. After her vision, there was nothing anyone could do to console her, it was like she was slowly losing her mind. She would stare at a wall without blinking for hours or become so focused on something that the only way to get her to stop was by shaking her. Without proper guidance and training Dad was afraid that Deme would lose herself entirely, so he booked the first plane ticket he could to Greece, so they could search for the Oracle that was rumored to be in hiding after the Romans and the French raided and ransacked the Temple of Apollo at Delphi.

I haven't heard from them since they left.

Aside from the few wolves, the only ones who stayed in Paradise were Aphrodite and Gabby. Gabby, because there was no way she was going to convince her mom to let her go on a road trip to search for help in the impending war, and Aphrodite stayed to protect her. And while Andrew did talk to Gabby on a regular basis, it was only to say how much they missed each other and hardly to talk about anything that was going on in the world.

So, the news was the only way I had any idea what was going on back home, and I hardly had a moment to myself to be able to do that. Any time Zagreus caught me, he would turn off whatever device I had obtained and tell me that I needed to focus on our mission rather than what was happening back home; and it *really* ticked me off when he did that. He even took my phone and has it hidden somewhere, although I haven't really gone looking for it either.

The door behind me clicks open and closed. For a split second, I hope that it's someone from the room next door to ours, but thanks to my "super wolf hearing" I know who it is by the sound of their footsteps. Zagreus' hands grip the iron wrought fencing and he lets out a long sigh. I distract myself by watching a leaf float along the murky pool water... It's crazy how one season can look in one state and look completely different in another. I miss the snow back home and the rain; winter just isn't the same outside of Paradise. There are thick green rings around the rim of the pool, and I can't decipher if its mold or algae over the overwhelming scent of Zagreus' cologne next to me. It's like a thick cloud of his scent is engulfing me, beckoning me to come closer to him. Zagreus is saying something, I know he is because the sound of his voice melts together with the sounds of the world. I don't want to hear what he is saying, I don't want to be here anymore. I want to go home. The setting sun reflects across the murky water, the leaf I was watching gets sucked into a pool filter that probably hasn't been cleaned since before summer.

"Rose, are you even listening to me?" He asks.

"Yes." I lie.

He turns to me and crosses his arms, "Then what was I saying?" I roll my eyes and let out a sigh.

"Doesn't matter." I state, "It's almost sunset, we need to get packed and back on the road. *Stick to the plan*, you know?" I brush past him towards the door, but I don't move as quickly as I can. I want him to stop me. I want him to grab my wrist, turn me around and make me face him. Make me hear him out. But he doesn't move, so I go inside the room and let the door close behind me.

"Someone better get me a jacket, a cold front just blew in" Andrew teases, stretching his arms out above him. I scowl at him and lock myself in the bathroom.

When my mom died, it was like we all died with her.

Dad, Nix, Deme, and me, we all just split apart. Grieving in our own separate ways. Each day felt like a knife was being wedged between us, urging us to get farther and farther apart until the knife cut the very binds that held us together.

I was already seeing a therapist for my memory loss when she got sick. I begged my parents to stop going, I wanted to stay home with mom, to help make her feel better. When she died, I kept going, hoping that one day I might have some more memories of her that I could hold onto.

It's been almost an entire year since I recovered my memories, but I still feel like I have a hole in my heart. One that keeps growing bigger, the longer my family is separated. It was Christmas the day we separated. With everything that was going on, somehow, we all forgot the one Holiday that was always the most important. As we approach the new year, it gets harder and harder to go on without talking to them, without seeing them.

The hole in my heart just wants to be home.

"Seriously, what is with you guys?" Andrew asks me. We're at a gas station, I'm not sure where but I'm pretty sure its somewhere in Oklahoma. I haven't been paying much attention, but the temperature is in the negatives and the gas station is covered in a thick layer of ice, so much that I was surprised that Zagreus was able to go inside. We had to pull into the station to take cover from the ice storm that came out of nowhere. Although with the fires burning in Arizona and the random storms plaguing the weather here, if I had to guess, I'd say it was the work of an angry god.

"What do you mean?" I ask him, pulling my jacket tighter against my chest.

"You know exactly what I mean."

"Nope. No idea." I lie.

"Rose, we have been best friends since early childhood, I know when you're lying to me."

"How?" I turn around in my seat and narrow my eyes at him.

"You always shake your head a little bit as you do it. It's like your body is telling the truth even if your mouth isn't." He explains. "Now tell me the truth."

"Fine," I roll my eyes, "We had a *moment*, and then my little sister had a vision about the end of the world and the moment passed. That's it."

"But you wish that it hadn't?" He asks.

"Hadn't what?"

"Passed. You wish the moment hadn't passed." He clarifies.

"What makes you say that?"

"I can just tell. Really? Stop playing dumb, Rose. If there is anyone here that knows you better than you know yourself, it's me." He says smugly and leans back into the backseat. A noise outside the car makes me jump, but it's just Zagreus starting the gas pump. I roll the window down a little to ask him something, but a cold burst of wind hits my face like a punch, and I roll it back up quickly. A moment later Zagreus hops back into the drivers' seat and shudders.

"Where are we?" I shiver, the cold that came in from his open door wrapping around me.

"Wichita falls." Zagreus answers.

"Where are we headed next?" Andrew asks, "Somewhere warmer, I hope."

"New Orleans" Zagreus answers flatly.

"What happened to Morganville?" I ask him.

"Apparently, it doesn't exist. Nobody has heard of it, and it isn't on any maps. So, we drive as far as we can before sunrise, rest for the day and repeat until we get to New Orleans. But it's only a nine-hour drive so we should make it there before sunrise."

"What's in New Orleans?" Andrew asks.

"Not what, *who*. And I don't even know if they're still there, so for now it doesn't matter."

"What do you mean?" I ask, "What is the point of driving all over the country if we don't even know if they are there for sure or not?" Zagreus turns to face me directly in his seat. His face so close to mine that I can feel the warmth radiating from his skin.

"Because the whole point of the original fight against Ares, was that my kind and anyone like us couldn't interfere in human lives anymore so, every single one of us went into hiding. No one knows where anyone is for sure." He sighs and sinks back into his seat, "All we have to go on is rumors."

"Why can't we use your portals to get there?" Andrew inquires.

"My *portals*?" Zagreus rubs his forehead. He looks exhausted.

"Yeah, you know—" Andrew claps his hands together, presses them against the center console and begins shaking the jeep—"Portals." I hide my laugh behind my hands, trying to play it off like I'm cold. Zagreus looks at me out of the corner of his eyes.

"Because the *portals* only lead to and from the underworld, and I don't think you want to have to go back and forth between the underworld every time we decide to go somewhere new." Zagreus explains.

"Oh." Andrew says defeated. Zagreus starts the car and pulls out of the station back onto the highway. Andrew settles back into his seat, pulling out his headphones and connecting them, in seconds his head is bobbing to the beat. I fiddle with the bracelet on my wrist as Zagreus begins to pick up speed and weaves in and out of the other cars on the road. Neither of us say anything to each other the rest of the car ride.

We pull into the parking lot of the next hotel we are staying at just as the sun begins to rise. I'm not entirely sure what I expected New Orleans to look like, but it wasn't this. At first, it felt like we hadn't even left Paradise. The trees and greenery flashing by in the car window as we drove into the city, looked like the ones I'd grown up with. But as we got deeper into the city and the buildings grew taller than the trees, I couldn't help but feel like we'd gone through some kind of gateway and into a magical city. All the beautiful lights, the music so loud I can hear it perfectly through the car windows, and the people laughing and partying on the sidewalks, heading home after a long night, I can't wait to be out there, experiencing it all. We haven't even parked the car yet and I already feel like I need to be here; like some unknown force is pulling me in and telling me to stay. That whatever we are looking for, is right here in this city, waiting for us to find it.

As Zagreus talks to the receptionist of the hotel, Andrew and I wait near the car taking in all the scenery around us. We haven't been staying in any one place for too long, just long enough to find out if what we needed was there and if not, we were on the road within the hour or headed out at nightfall. Christmas day we made it halfway through New Mexico, Zagreus said that there was a chance we might find "The Minotaur of the Mountain" but that turned out to be a mud run some town was holding to raise money for charity. In Texas, we made our way to Athens, where we were following multiple leads about Dionysus living on a vineyard, although that turned out to be an even bigger waste of time than the Minotaur was. Texas was where we heard of a rumor that there was a strange town called Morganville, that for some reason, people couldn't remember anything about. So, Zagreus thought it might be the work of Lethe, the Greek God of forgetfulness and oblivion, of course it was probably some drunk townie who had a little too much to drink and couldn't remember hitching a ride out of town or something.

Every town, every state, every mile was a complete waste of time.

This hotel is a huge upgrade compared to all the lousy motels we've been staying in the last couple of days. It's a huge building, with well over a hundred rooms, a giant chandelier, and a grand piano in the lobby and from what I can see as we make our way to the elevator, a gorgeous pool. It would take me days maybe even weeks, to explore every inch of this place.

When we get to the room, I'm shocked even more. It's a suite, with a kitchen, living area and two separate rooms. I move past the boys and over to the window to find an incredible view of what looks like the entire city.

"That's the Mississippi River over there." Zagreus points out the window towards a huge bridge in the distance.

"Are we really staying here?" I ask.

"Yeah, why wouldn't we?"

"We've been staying in some of the worst motels in the U.S. and now it's like were staying in a castle. What gives?"

"Nothing gives. New Orleans was always one of our major stopping points, so why not be more comfortable if we are going to be here for a while?" He explains.

"How long are we going to be here?" I ask.

"I don't really know. I mean it's a huge city, it could take us a while to track down all these leads." Zagreus walks over to one of the leather couches and sits down. "Plus, I'll probably have to go restock on Andrew food soon and I'd rather not force him to sleep in a blanket fort when he's starving. You know?"

"Hey! I liked that blanket fort." Andrew calls out from one of the rooms.

"Better than these beds? Cause we can build you another one and I'll take the bed!" Zagreus calls back to him, raising an eyebrow at me.

"No! no—this is better. Way better." Andrew concedes.

"That's what I thought." He chuckles, "Rose why don't you check out the other room, I'll crash on the couch this time." I pick up my duffle bag from the floor and head over to the door on the other side of the suite and throw it open. There's something about being in a hotel room that makes me want to run across the room and belly flop onto the perfectly made bed, I've never fully understood why, but I've also never resisted. I land perfectly in the middle of the bed and bounce to turn over, letting the thick white comforter engulf me.

I wake up almost an hour later, the sun now fully in the sky and shining down on the world outside of my window. I pull myself out of bed and into the bathroom before I remember that I passed out before I unpacked. I reach for my duffle bag by the bedroom door and realize the entire suite is silent. The blinds are drawn in the living area for Andrew's sake, and I don't see any movement. Zagreus isn't on the couch either, but not bothering to wonder where he is, I pull my bag into the room and close the door. I pull off my sweats that I wore for the car ride and slip into a pair of jeans and an emerald green, cable knit sweater. I brush my hair, brush my teeth, and put on some mascara before pulling my shoes from under the bed. I slip out of my room as quietly as I can, grab a room-key from the counter and go out to explore.

The streets are busy. With people and cars buzzing all around. I take a deep breath, pick a direction, and begin walking. I walk at least a mile, not sure where my feet are taking me, until I find myself walking down Bourbon Street. The amount of people here compared to a lot of the other streets is breathtaking. There are people playing instruments, people with live snakes offering to let you take pictures with them, pizza places, steakhouses, cabarets, bars, and clothing shops. The architecture is incredible, all along the narrow street, each building has a balcony that overlooks it, with flags and lights strewn along the banisters. But the smells are what keep pulling me down the street, it smells like nothing I have ever encountered before.

Delicious and sweet, savory and delectable. I walk for miles and miles as the sun sets above me. I grab a coffee from a café and sip on it as I admire the sights. I don't know where I'm going, just taking it all in, one step at a time.

I have never been in a city like this before. Sometimes back home we would take trips to Mesa to go shopping or have fancy dinner. But more than often, we would travel to the city for school field trips. We went to the zoo more times I can remember, but we also took a trip to the Grand Canyon and another to a Chinese festival around new year. But the buildings in Arizona are different. I know it's mostly because they build them to match their surroundings, but the dull cream colors and burnt red on the bridges is nothing compared to the architectural design in the brick work on some of the buildings here in New Orleans. The culture runs deep here, something that I don't think you will ever see back home in Arizona or maybe even in a few other States that we have been to these last few days.

It's not until the sun has almost set, that I stop. I've been walking through the city for hours. There is a big brick building in front of me, with an intricate iron gate wrapped in vines of some kind and a big, rusted M is welded onto it. I stare up at the building. Most of the buildings and houses around me have a short front stoop that is very close to the street, but this building is set very far back from the street. With a long walkway of patterned masonry surrounded by flowers and trees I have never seen, the textured walls are white and the ornamental brackets a brilliant gold. The lights are on inside, but all the curtains are closed and I'm not sure why, but I can't make myself walk away from it; like this is why I'm here, this is where I need to be. I reach for the gate and just before I push it open a hand on my shoulder startles me and I jump forward, turning around I find myself face to face with Zagreus.

2

Medusa

"Rose, What the hell were you *thinking*?" Zagreus grabs me by shoulders and pulls me into him. "I've been looking for you everywhere." I don't say anything, for some reason this exchange makes me feel like a child. He lets go of me and takes a step back. "Why did you run off like that?" now he's *talking* to me like a child.

"I didn't." I tell him.

"I left to get Andrew more—" He looks around, a group of people across the street are staring. "More food. And when I got back, you were just gone. You didn't leave a note or anything."

"Well, if you didn't take my phone, I would've been able to call." I tell him, his face falls.

"Okay, maybe—" He looks around again. "Maybe we shouldn't be talking about this here." He furrows his brow as he looks around, "Where is here anyway?"

"I don't know, I was just walking and something about this place drew me in." I turn back to the building; all the lights are now turned off. "That's weird."

"What is?"

"The lights, they... never mind." I turn back to him. "Should we go back to the hotel then?" I ask.

"At the very least, we need to go get Andrew. Since the suns down, he can come out. I thought we would do some sight-seeing together."

"Can't do much sight-seeing at night. Most of the tourist stuff closes." I tell him, he looks disappointed again.

"We could go to a museum in the morning if you'd like. Just next time you want to explore, let someone know where you are going. I thought something happened." He offers.

"I'm not a baby, Zagreus. I'm barely even human, I can take care of myself." I tell him, "Let's go get Andrew." I don't know if it is because neither of us knew what to say to the other or if he is still mad at me, but we walk back to the hotel together in silence. All I can think about is that brick building. Why, of all places, did I stop there? Was that why I felt so drawn to this city? Was there something there that we needed? There were too many unanswered questions. I needed to go back.

Andrew is waiting for us in the lobby when we reach the hotel.

"Hey! What took you guys so long?" He asks.

I look up at Zagreus, then back at Andrew. "Sorry, my fault. I went a little farther than I thought."

"Oh, that's okay." He pats me on the shoulder, "I'm starving though, let's go get some grub." He pulls my hand to turn me around, I look at Zagreus for reassurance. He shrugs and follows us back out the big glass doors.

We find a fancy steakhouse a couple streets down the road.

"Are you sure we can afford this?" I ask.

"Oh, come on. Don't we deserve to live a little? We've had nothing but fast food the last couple days." Andrew gives me a puppy dog face.

"We can afford it." Zagreus states. We get sat at a tiny square table and order drinks, when the waiter walks away Andrew almost moans at the menu.

"All of this sounds so good!" He exclaims.

"That's because you have a bottomless pit for a stomach. You could eat everything on the menu and still be hungry." I joke, Andrew gives me a dirty look.

"And what are you going to get? A salad." He mocks, this time I give him a dirty look. We finish looking over the menu and order; Andrew and Zagreus both get steak, medium rare for Zagreus, rare for Andrew, while I go for a marinated and roasted chicken breast. It's a beautiful restaurant, not like any that I've been to before. I did see one like this on an episode of kitchen nightmares though, although this place looked like the after pictures instead of the before.

"I think we need to set some ground rules." Zagreus tells us after we get our food.

"Ground rules?" Andrew asks with his mouth full.

"Yes, ground rules." He gives Andrew a weird look. "No more running around like this is Paradise. You both are in a brand-new place; you don't know where you're going, and you could get lost or worse. So, from now on, no one goes anywhere alone."

"Sounds fair." Andrew says.

Speak for yourself.

Zagreus looks at me, waiting for me to agree.

"Sure, fine. It won't happen again." I tell shrug at him. He raises his eyebrows at me, "I mean it, Z. I won't go anywhere on my own again. Scouts honor." I hold my hand to my chest.

"You shook your head." Andrew mumbles under his breath. I kick him under the table and glare at him when Zagreus takes a sip of his coffee.

"Next, you guys should know what we're here for." Zagreus goes on. "There haven't been many leads as to where we can find anyone willing to help us. But I heard from Aph—" He looks around, no one seems to be paying us any mind. "—rodite, that there was a group of Gorgons living somewhere in New Orleans. Now, they're probably not going to be too excited about us showing up and might even—"

"Wait, like turn you to stone gorgons?" I ask a little too loudly, the table to the right of us gives me a weird look. I give my best apologetic look to them.

"Yes, Rose. The very same." Zagreus rubs his temple. "Anyway, they might try to flee or hurt us if we try to pursue them, but Medusa doesn't like the other gods too much. So, there might be a chance we get her on our side." Medusa. Living in New Orleans, what are the odds?

"But wasn't she killed?" Andrew asks, "like beheaded." He holds his knife up to his throat and mimics slicing it.

"At one point yes. But Athena saw to it that she was restored."

"Got it." Andrew says between mouthfuls.

"*Restored?*" I ask.

"Yeah, I don't really know much about it to be honest. It isn't often that someone gets brought back from the Underworld, but it does happen."

M. There was a big metal M on the gate of the house I went to earlier. Could that be Medusa? Would she really draw that much attention to herself?

"I also, wanted to give this back." Zagreus pulls something out of his pocket and slides it across the table to me. It's my phone. "I kept it charged in case your family called. But I need you to promise me that you won't get to upset about what you might see on the news. We can't go home, not yet. The best thing we can do is try to stop Ares, that is the only way we can save Paradise."

"Thanks." I take my phone from the table, turn the screen on and shove it in my pocket. No missed calls or texts. No new notifications at all.

I stare at my phone where it rests on the edge of the bed, willing for it to ring; but it doesn't. The phone calls never come. Maybe I should call, but I don't know what time it is in Greece, and I don't even know if Nix has his phone wherever he is. I could call Gabby, or Aphrodite, just to hear their voices; to feel a little bit of home when I'm so far from it. But I leave it on the edge of the bed. I pull the blankets up around me and take a deep breath. It's well past midnight now and Zagreus and I are supposed to be up early to go look around the city and try to find some clues as to where the gorgons are, but I can't sleep.

Instead, I cry.

Hot tears fall down my face and land on the white sheets of the hotel bed. They fall like a storm that surrounds me in the forest, slow at first and then enough to make the rivers rise and the leaves shake. I cry so hard my throat begins to hurt, and my cheeks burn. There is no point in wiping my face, no sense in pretending that I am not crying, there is no stopping this storm.

I cry for Gabby, who never would have known about the gods or the end of the world if it wasn't for me. I cry for Andrew, who became a vampire because of me. I cry for my mother, who will never get to watch her children grow old with the man she loves. I cry for my dad, who crumbled under the pressures of my mom dying and raising three supernatural children without her. I cry for Phoenix, who lived so many years alone in a dungeon, only to be thrown into a life that didn't belong to him anymore. I cry for Deme, whose mind doesn't really belong to her anymore, and how she will never have a normal life again. And lastly, I cry for me, because of everything I have been through the last year and how none of it will be for anything if we don't stop Ares. Because I lost my memories and wanted them back so badly, it was my entire personality. Because I was sexually assaulted at a party. Because I was almost killed by a chimera. Because my best friend got trapped in the underworld and came back as something unhuman. Because I almost killed Zagreus' sister. Because I fell in love with a boy who turned out to be a Greek god and none of this would be happening if he just never came back into my life.

I don't want to be here anymore. I want to be home, snuggled in my bed and listening to the sounds of my family in the rooms around mine. I didn't ask for this, any of it. I can't do this anymore. I won't do this anymore.

The door opens slowly, and someone walks in. He quietly sits down at the end of the bed but doesn't say a word. He lets me cry in silence for a few minutes. His familiar scent engulfs me, Teakwood, cinnamon, vanilla. I don't want him to see me like this; weak and vulnerable. I want to say something, anything, to show him I'm not. I want to be strong and invincible, to carry my burdens without conviction. But I'm full of silence, one I don't know how to break. He gets up, moves to the side of the bed, and pulls back the blankets before crawling under them with me and wrapping his arms around my curled-up body. His warmth engulfing me and calming my shaking limbs, he holds me until the only evidence of my sadness is the tear-stained sheets.

The bed next to me is empty in the morning. The sheets, pillow and comforter look like they were never moved. Like no one was there in the first place. I close my eyes, remembering what it felt like to have Zagreus' arms wrapped around me. The warmth of his body against mine. I shake my head and get up, making my way to the bathroom to get ready for whatever he has planned for the rest of the day. Maybe I should tell him about the things I was feeling and that I want to go home. But he hasn't been the best listener since we left, and he will probably just blow me off again. I guess I'm just along for the ride.

We get breakfast at the hotel, take a short walk around the building for some fresh air, and then get started around the city. We go to museums and small shops, taking in all the culture and beautiful scenery around us. He doesn't bring up last night, and neither do I, instead he slows his pace when I look through the window of a shop we pass or takes his time reading a sign when I begin to lose my breath so I can rest. Zagreus takes his time with me, showing me all of the beauty of this city, distracting me from my own thoughts. But another thing that bothers me is the gold and white building with the big metal "M" on the gate. Could it really be Medusa, could she really be that obvious? And why didn't Zagreus mention it? Maybe he didn't see the gate, he could have just been so worried about where I'd gone that he wasn't looking for anything else. But should I mention it to him, or should I try to go back alone?

We stop for lunch at a random shop on Bourbon Street. Zagreus goes over the menu and orders us both a sandwich and a coke, but I can't help but feel uneasy. Like someone in this place is watching us. Behind the check-out counter, the employee pays us no mind, but at a booth across the room I lock eyes with a man before he looks back down at his newspaper; maybe I'm just being paranoid.

"Do you know how your sister is doing?" I ask Zagreus, he looks up at me confused.

"What?"

"Melinoe, is she doing better?"

"I assume so." He furrows his brows, "Rose, you don't need to worry about her. She would have killed you without a second thought."

I sit back in my seat, "I know," I whisper, *I know better than anyone.*

"Good." He takes a sip of his coke and clears his throat, "Is there something bothering you?" He asks.

"No." I shake my head slightly, now that I know I have a tell when I'm lying, I keep catching myself doing it. "Okay maybe. But I don't know, it's probably nothing."

"If it's bothering you, then it isn't nothing." He reaches across the table and takes my hand in his, "you can tell me."

"It's just, that house." I start, "The one that you found me at yesterday."

"What about it?" He asks, he looks confused, like this isn't what he expected me to say.

"I feel like..." I take a deep breath, "I feel like something is calling me to it, like I need to be there for some odd reason. Like its everything that we've been looking for."

"Okay," He takes what I said in for a moment, looks down at his empty plate and back up at me, "So let's go." He squeezes my hand, "Together."

I'm not sure why, but for some reason being here with Zagreus makes me more nervous about this place than I did when I came here alone. As we slowly make our way to the gate, I get more anxious with every step until we are standing in front of the big metal gate. The odd thing is, that the metal M on the center of the gate is no longer rusted, instead it is bright gold, shimmering in the sunlight.

"Rose, do you know what this place could be?" Zagreus asks me.

"Yes." I swallow, "I didn't know at first, but after you told us why we were here, I put it all together." I explain.

I reach forward for the gate, "Rose wait, it could be—" Zagreus starts but I ignore him and push the gate open, "—a trap." He finishes, but he sounds distracted. Zagreus walks in ahead of me but he stops every few steps to touch one of the plants along the walkway and mutter something to himself.

"Are you okay?" I ask him.

"Yeah." He says distantly. "It's just that," he shakes his head, "well some of these plants I haven't seen in a really long time." He explains, "Like this one—," He points to a small flower with green leaves and pale pink-grey-white flowers just starting to bloom, "This is asphodel." He smiles, "But they shouldn't be blooming right now, let alone they shouldn't even be here. But none of these plants should be blooming right now, most of them aren't even in season, and half of them don't bloom at the same time of year as the others." He explains to me, still sounding a million miles away from me. I don't think I have ever seen Zagreus this excited over plants, or maybe even anything. He is so excited about the flowers that he doesn't notice the figure standing in the doorway of the ornate building, staring straight at us.

To be fair, I wouldn't have noticed them either if their eyes weren't glowing.

"Zagreus." I tap him on the shoulder urgently. He looks at me, his expression confused then realizing as he snaps up and covers my eyes.

"Don't look at them!" He shouts, but I hear a chuckle coming from the direction of the figure.

"We have been expecting you." The figure speaks, although I'm assuming it's the figure since Zagreus is still covering my eyes, "Follow me." She commands before adding, "And don't be ridiculous, I will not turn you to stone no matter how much I might want to." I hear her footsteps recede into the building and Zagreus uncovers my face before we follow her into the building.

The inside of the building is much more intricate with the details than it is on the outside. The flooring is made of marble, but in the center of the foyer there is a dark green circle of marbling that upon closer inspection, looks like two snakes entwined together with golden branches. There are columns holding up the second story that look like they were hand carved, and artwork on the walls that looks like it came from my history book. I am completely blown away by the sheer cost of what it must have taken to build a quarter of this building, let alone the rest of it.

"The House of Miss Duza has been around for hundreds of years, and she has been a pillar of this community for most of them. However, I must ask that you keep your knowledge of this place to a secret. If word got out, it could be catastrophic for all those involved." Something about the woman's tone tells me that it would be explicitly catastrophic for Zagreus and me, not for anyone else, but I remain quiet. The woman is tall, dark skinned with a golden tint that glitters in the light and her hair is wrapped in a red headwrap, tied at the top in a knot. Her nails are filed into a sharp point and painted golden, and she is wearing a long red gown that covers her body from the neck down. She has an accent too, although I can't place where it's from.

"That's Stheno." Zagreus whispers to me. I try to rack my brain to remember anything about Stheno from Greek mythology but the only thing I can remember about her is that she is one of the sisters of Medusa. She leads us to an office that is decorated in all kinds of golds and greens, with a large dark wood desk in the center of the room and strange artifacts on the shelves behind it. Stheno instructs us to wait here.

"Who is Stheno?" I ask Zagreus when she leaves the room and shuts the door.

"She is the sister of Medusa. But she is also a ruthless killer." Zagreus tells me, "She has killed more men than any of her siblings combined." I can't help but think that some of those men probably deserved it.

"Should we have waited?" I ask him.

"For what?" Zagreus whispers.

"For Andrew maybe, I don't know. I feel bad leaving him in the room for all of this."

"Your vampire will be fine" A voice behind us announces, causing me to jump in my seat. A beautiful woman is standing in the doorway that Stheno left through. She is tall, with similar skin to her sister, only darker. Before I can think not to, I notice that her eyes are different colors, mainly blue, but with specks and swirls of reds and greens. She is also wearing a golden headwrap covering her hair and a matching gold gown. Her presence, however, doesn't make me feel uneasy, she makes me feel welcome; like she was the one I was waiting for all along. "I was wondering when you would show up." She says to me with a slight smile on her lips.

"You must be—" Zagreus starts.

"Medusa." Her gaze quickly shifts to him as he speaks to her, "You, however, I was not expecting." She looks angry with him.

"I'm sorry, ma'am we're just here to—" I start but she cuts me off too.

"I know why you are here." Her gaze returns to mine, and she looks kinder again, "But you are also here for other reasons. Reasons you do not yet know." She rounds the desk and stands on the other side. "So, you must have questions, yes?"

"What is this place?" I ask before Zagreus can say anything.

She smiles, "This is the House of Miss Duza. It is a sanctuary for women, for people of color, and it becomes whatever they need, whenever they need it. And it can only be found by those who require my assistance. But more commonly, The House of Miss Duza is a home for survivors."

"Survivors?"

"The world is not kind to women, my dear, and it is much worse to people of my skin tone." Her facial expression seems sincere, but I can see hurt behind her eyes. She sits behind the desk and folds her hands together on the dark wood. "I was a devout woman back in the early times, but men can sometimes feel threatened by a woman who is so sure of herself that they will do *anything* to break her. I was broken and given the ultimate gift of protection by Athena. The power to turn anyone who wrongs me to stone. Then I was once again hunted and beheaded by man because of this gift. It was in the Underworld, the realm of your fathers—," she gestures to Zagreus, "Where the spirits first spoke to me, and where I was given a second chance by Persephone to return to the land of the living to heal those in need."

"My mother. Not Athena?" Zagreus asks.

"Yes, your mother. Sometimes, when a story is spread by many people, details get muddied and those who want the credit, take it. You should know this better than any, young god." She explains to Zagreus, I'm not sure exactly what she is talking about, but he doesn't say anything.

"But how did you get here? Why New Orleans?" I ask her.

"Like I said, the world has not been kind to black women. I was stolen, and sold, enslaved, and put to work for nothing in return." The red specks in her eyes grow larger, she takes a deep breath, and they return to normal. "The only thing I got out of it, was the chance to disappear from the eyes of the gods who abandoned me."

"But couldn't you have just turned them to stone? The men who enslaved you." I ask.

"Of course, but I would have been killed again, burned at the stake for witchcraft or vodou by the others. It was much simpler to live through it, to learn from it and to assist those around me who needed it. To teach the way of healing to my friends, to the people who did not have a gift to help themselves in the first place. We are still fighting many battles against those who judge on skin tone, I am needed here, where those who need my help will find it."

"So, you won't help us?" I ask her, she smiles sweetly at me.

"Not in the way you would like me to dear girl." She stands up and smooths her dress down, "Now, let us take a walk in the gardens." Zagreus and I stand up with her, but she shakes her finger at him, "Not you boy, just the girl and I." At first, he doesn't move, his eyes darting between the two of us, as if he is trying to decide whether or not to whisk us both out of here.

"I'll be fine Zagreus." I reach out and squeeze his hand and smile.

"Yes, we will only be gone a moment. Stheno will bring you something to replenish with if you wish. I'm afraid I font have any food worthy of a god, but I did just finish whipping up a pot of gumbo." Medusa winks at him and together we walk out of a door on the side of the room I didn't notice before.

The back gardens are much more lavish than I expected. There are more plants than I can name, marble fountains and ornate benches along a stone pathway that we walk down. Her pace is slow as she allows me to take in all the scenery.

"You hold yourself well." Medusa tells me.

"Thank you?" It comes out like a question because I don't really know what to say to this.

"You have been through so much."

Again, I don't really know what to say to her, "It was noth-ing." I squeak out.

"There is no need to be modest, you have scars that cannot be seen by others." She sits on one of the benches and pats the seat next to her. "I have the same scars. Ones that haunt you in your dreams, fears that you hide deep down in your subcon-scious. You and I have more in common than you might think."

I take a deep breath, "It hasn't been the easiest." I tell her, and before I know it, I'm telling her everything. It is like word vomit; the words just spill from my mouth one after the other.

Although I seem to be making sense, because Medusa doesn't interrupt to ask questions, she listens, occasionally nodding her head to let me know she is still listening. I tell her everything, from my family to Andrew and Zagreus, to all the pain I feel, to what happened with Tyler and everything leading up to now. And I don't cry this time. I don't shed a single tear as I feel all these things again, and I let myself feel them, I let her feel the pain along with me. I didn't even share this much with my therapist when I first met him, I made him work for the hard stuff. But with Medusa its easy, like she is my mother or a best friend I've known my whole life. "And that is everything, I think." I look up and she smiles at me, reaches for my hand and squeezes.

"Such an unfair life for such a beautiful young girl." She responds, "But I know this journey has only just begun and there is going to be so much more for you to go through. But this is what makes you strong." She sighs, "I sense that you are still afraid."

"Afraid of what?" I ask her.

"Afraid of loving." She states sincerely, "You have been hurt at the hands of man, don't let this keep you from loving, don't let this moment take your life from you." She says, "Did you know that when a god takes you as his mate, that makes you his or hers for life?" She asks me.

"I didn't."

"He is letting you make the choice."

"He?"

She chuckles a little, "The young god, the one you came here with. Zagreus is letting you make the choice because he doesn't want to take that away from you. Like that Tyler did with you, or like Poseidon did with me." She closes her eyes for a moment, "Poseidon and I are linked eternally, and I will never find another love because of what he took from me. But that boy, the one eagerly waiting for your return, the one who cares so deeply for you but won't show it, he will not take the decision from you. You must choose him if that is what you want." She must see the confusion on my face, "Although you do not need to make the decision now, nor anytime soon. I just thought you ought to know that Zagreus will wait for you till the end if he must."

I smile softly, "Thank you. It was nice to be able to talk to someone without thinking they are going to judge me."

"No need to thank me, everyone deserves to be able to share how they feel without judgement. It is how you found me, and it will be how others find me as well." She squeezes my hand again, "Now we should get back to young Zagreus before he decides to come looking for us." I hadn't noticed, but the sun was setting, I've been outside with Medusa for hours. I nod and we head back inside, to the office where Zagreus is still waiting for me.

When we get back to the office, Zagreus looks worried until I give him a reassuring smile and he relaxes a little. He stands to meet me at the door and Medusa walks us back to the main lobby where Stheno is still waiting. "Before you go," Medusa starts, "I told you I would not help you in the way that you want, but I will tell you this," She stands still for a moment, "You can find the god of the sea in South Carolina, on the coast at a place called Port Royal." She states.

"*Sister*," Stheno hisses.

"Oh hush," She tells her, "He likes to frequent the bars in that area, it shouldn't be difficult to locate him."

"How do you know this? No one has heard from him or Zeus since the war with Ares." Zagreus asks her, narrowing his eyes.

"Never mind how I know, I just do." She winks at me, "But you should stay in New Orleans another night, there is no better place to ring in the new year." Medusa smiles. "And do be sure to dress for the occasion."

"Thank you," I tell her.

"Remember what I said Rose and do take care." She hugs me tightly. We say our goodbyes and Zagreus and I walk out the front doors and out onto the porch.

"What did she tell you?" Zagreus asks as we walk back down to the street, through all the plants that distracted him on the way in.

"It doesn't matter much, she mostly just listened to me." I tell him.

"What did you tell her?"

I shrug, "Everything."

"Everything?" He exclaims as we shut the gate behind us.

"It all kind of just came out, I don't know why. But it was nice talking to someone." I tell him.

"Maybe just give Doctor Foster a call next time, I was really worried she was going to make you into her next garden gnome out there." He tells me.

"Why were we able to look them in the eyes?" I ask, "I thought we couldn't even make eye contact with them, or they would turn us to stone."

"Well yeah, that's the myth. But it's up to them if they deem you a threat to their safety or not."

"I guess that makes sense." I look back at the building, only to find that its gone, "Oh,"

"What?" Zagreus turns to me and notices the building is gone too. "I guess that's what Medusa meant when she said that she can only be found by someone who needs her."

"Yeah, I guess so." I stare at the empty lot for a moment.

I guess I don't need her anymore.

Cosmic Love

"You met WHO?" Andrew shouts at us back in the hotel room. "Man, I miss everything good." He adds.

"Sorry, it just kind of happened." I tell him.

"And to be fair she only wanted to talk to Rose anyway." Zagreus adds not bothering to look up from his phone. He is looking for a good restaurant to eat dinner at; he's already called three but couldn't get in because of how busy it is for new year's.

"What did you guys talk about? Tell me everything." Andrew gives me his full attention, crossing his legs and facing me on the couch.

"She apparently told her *everything*" Zagreus tells him, I roll my eyes.

"What is everything?" Andrew asks skeptically.

"Just everything we've been through, from the very beginning to now." I explain.

"Wow, way to hold back." Andrew says.

"Yeah, well it seemed like she already knew every-thing anyway. She didn't even ask us our names and she knew that you are a vampire." I tell him, I notice that he cringes when I call him a vampire.

"That can't be it though, I mean did she say anything to you?" Andrew asks.

"I mean not really," I try to give him a look that says *I'll-explain-more-when-were-alone* but I don't think he gets it.

"How could she have not said anything." He asks.

Zagreus gets up and puts his phone to his ear. "Yeah, do you have any openings?" He asks whoever is on the other line.

I scoot closer to Andrew and whisper, "She told me that when a god makes you his mate, you belong to him for life." Andrew raises his eyes as if he's about to yell something, so I cover his mouth. "I don't want him to know that I know. So, shush." He rolls his eyes and pulls my hand away from his mouth.

"Great! We will be there!" Zagreus exclaims and hangs up the phone. "I got us a reservation." He shakes the phone in victory, "So what were you talking about?"

"I was just telling him that Medusa told us where to find Poseidon." I quickly tell Zagreus before Andrew can say anything.

"I don't know about that," Zagreus says.

"What do you mean?" I ask him.

"I mean that she doesn't have the best history with him, why would she be the only one to know where he is?" Zagreus asks us.

"Well, I mean, wouldn't you try to always know where some-one who once hurt you is? That way you could avoid them." Andrew answers him, I just look at him. "What? I can be smart sometimes." He shrugs.

"I guess that makes sense, I mean it's as good a guess as any. We might as well check it out." Zagreus shrugs, "Now, its New Year's Eve, we are in New Orleans, and we have a dinner reservation in about an hour, so go get ready. I don't want to be late." He kicks us off the couch and to our rooms.

Waiting on the bed in my room is three black boxes. Each box has each of our names written in gold across the top, one for Zagreus, Andrew, and me. I open the one with my name and there is a gold M sticker on the tissue paper holding whatever it is the box contains. I carefully open the tissue paper and pull out a glamorous red dress, I look at it for a moment and put it back in the box and carry the other two out to the living room of the suite. Zagreus is still on the couch, he looks up and sees me carrying the two boxes, "What are those?" He asks getting up to help me.

"Gifts from Medusa." I tell him, he raises an eyebrow and I hear Andrew fumbling with the door to his room before peeking his head out.

"Did you just say gifts from Medusa?" Andrew asks, I hold out his box to him, and he practically falls over running over to me. He grabs the box and Zagreus grabs his, and I leave them to get dressed.

In my own room I pull the dress back out and hang it from the back of the door. It is a deep red, floor length, spaghetti-strap dress with a V-neck I'm not sure I can pull off. There are also black strappy heels and some gold necklaces and bracelets in the box. Seeing everything picked out like this reminds me of my sister trying to dress me for that party so long ago. I shake off the thought and I do my makeup first, trying to channel my little sister's skill with liquid eyeliner and gold shimmering eyeshadows, finishing off the look with the darkest red lipstick I own. As for my hair I leave it curled and down, hanging loosely around my shoulders. I slip on the dress and look in the mirror, it fits me perfectly even with the back not being fully zipped, I'm going to have to ask one of the boys to finish zipping it up for me. I look over at the strappy heels and groan. I've never particularly liked wearing heels. My sister and I used to raid my mothers' closet and run around in her heels to make her laugh but other than that I don't have much experience wearing them. I know my feet are going to hurt after this. It takes me more than a few minutes to get the shoes strapped just right and I wobble a little bit when I stand up, but I take a few laps around my room to get used to walking in them; let's just hope that there isn't carpet as thick as this wherever we're going. I pull out the jewelry from the box and look at them. One is a golden necklace with a small snake charm on it that I put on and it hangs perfectly in the V-neck of the dress, but the other is a snake bangle and since I'm already wearing the bracelet that Zagreus gave me with the wolf and moonstone on it, I decide to leave the bangle in the box.

I peek out of my door and Andrew is sitting on the couch, he has on a pair of black chino pants, an emerald-green button up shirt with a black jacket and dark dress shoes, he has come a long way from his dad's blue tuxedo that he wore to school dances. His locs are pulled back into a ponytail behind his head with a few loose strands that frame his face. I step out of my room, and he looks up at me. "Wow, Rosey! You look great!" He smiles.

"Thanks, so do you. But do you think you could help me zip this up the rest of the way?" I ask him as I point to the back of my dress. He stands up and I pull my hair to the side then pull the back of the dress down as he fiddles with the zipper. Andrew's door opens and out walks Zagreus, he looks great. He is wearing a similar outfit to Andrew, only his shirt is a dark red that matches the red of my dress perfectly. His hair is combed, but it's getting longer again, the sides of his head are still short, but the top has a perfect swoop to it that I'm not sure if he tried to achieve or if it just did it on its own. He pulls his jacket tight as he walks out the door and finally makes eye contact with me. He stops doing anything, like he's frozen in place. He looks me up and down, and I find myself blushing.

"Rose, you look—" Zagreus pauses, looking me up and down again, "You look beautiful." He smiles.

"Thank you, you look very handsome yourself." I blush.

"Hopefully we're not too overdressed for this restaurant." Andrew laughs.

"Probably not, but we should get going." Zagreus claps Andrew on the shoulder and we head out on the town.

If I was overwhelmed before by the amount of people, I couldn't tell you what I was now. As we walk up to the restaurant, we hold hands to make sure that we don't get separated because there are people everywhere and I mean everywhere. There are people on balconies, people in the streets, police officers on horses, live bands on the sidewalks, people walking down the street playing trumpets and other instruments, its breathtaking and terrifying, and beautiful all at the same time. The restaurant we walk into has a balcony that people are dancing on and throwing beads at the people in the streets, there is dance music playing loudly but quiets down as we make it to the host stand.

"Reservation Name?" The hostess asks, she is wearing a white button up with a red vest, dress pants and a black tie. Her black curly hair bounces as she talks.

"Areon Lux." Zagreus tells her. I get confused, and then remember that was the name he chose when we first met. She nods and beckons us to follow her. We are led to a table in the back corner of the restaurant, the table is decorated with lit candles, and the seats are a dark wood with white velvet cushions; this has got to be the fanciest place I have ever stepped foot in. Zagreus pulls my chair out for me before taking his own seat across from me and Andrew takes the one to the right of me. The waitress comes by and takes our orders and brings us each a glass of water. All around us, people are chatting and laughing and having an all-around good time, it feels good to be right in the middle of it all.

"Is there anything else here that we need to be looking for?" Andrew asks as he sips his water.

"Like what?" Zagreus asks him.

"Like I don't know, maybe a satyr of the strip or something." Andrew explains and Zagreus laughs.

"A satyr wouldn't be caught dead here." He keeps laughing.

"Why not?" I ask.

"They belong to nature, not cities. They listen to the music of the wind, not Cardi B."

"What's wrong with Cardi B?" Andrew asks him defensively.

"Yeah, and how exactly do *you* know who that is?" I add.

Zagreus glares at both of us, "You know, technically you both are older than me." He says smirking, "I just age faster." I stick my tongue out at him, and he laughs. The waitress brings over our appetizers, Oysters Rockefeller, and Gruyere and Crab Palmiers; things that I don't think I have ever had in my entire life. Both boys pick up an oyster, tap them together like they made a toast and then look at me.

"What?" I ask them.

"You aren't going to have one?" Andrew asks me.

"I don't think so, no." I shake my head.

"You have to." Zagreus tells me.

"No, I do not." I object.

"Okay, maybe you don't *have* to." Andrew rolls his eyes, "But you should."

"You just might like them." Zagreus picks one up and holds it out towards me. We lock eyes, neither backing down. Zagreus raises his eyebrows, smiles, and shakes the extra oyster in his hand, I relent.

"Fine." I take the oyster ashes both boys cheer and hold up their oysters again. "You guys are so lame." I laugh but I put mine in the air and we clink the shells together like we are taking a shot. They are a lot better than I thought they would be, sweet, and maybe a little salty, but the cheese *definitely* helps. As we get through the appetizers and the main course is brought out to us, it feels almost like home again. I feel happy.

"Okay, you have to tell me now. How can we keep eating out at fancy places and stay at fancy hotels?" I ask Zagreus as we finish eating.

"Well technically we aren't paying for the hotel suite." He says while wiping the corners of his mouth with his napkin. "Aphrodite owns it."

"She *owns* it?" I repeat.

"Yeah. A few of the god's own property like that all over the world." He explains. Andrew and I share a look of *is-this-guy-serious.*

"And how can the gods afford things like that?" Andrew asks.

"Well, I mean, gold has a high conversion rate and sacrifices and offerings used to be more common back in the day. It all adds up. You didn't think they all lived on Mount Olympus twenty-four-seven, did you?" Zagreus says nonchalantly.

"Yeah." Andrew and I say in unison, Zagreus laughs.

"Well, they don't. Some of us still have jobs to do. I mean, my mom brings the spring, Poseidon has his earthquakes, Zeus brings the storms, I mean I can go on about it all night." He explains.

"But I thought you said that Ares forced the gods to stop interfering?" Andrew asks.

"He did, but mostly with mortal lives. The world wouldn't be able to continue without our influence over it." The waitress drops off the bill, Zagreus pays, and we head back out onto the street.

"Did you guys want to go back to the hotel? Or we could make our way down to the water, I'm pretty sure that the Fleur-de-lis drop at midnight is down that way and we still have plenty of time until then." Zagreus asks us, there is still a huge crowd of people around us. I raise my eyebrow at him, "I might have looked it up." He explains.

"Let's go down, I'm sure it'll be a blast!" Andrew yells over the passing crowd. I nod in agreement, and we follow Zagreus through the crowd and down to the waterfront.

On the way to the waterfront, we pass by a bar with live music playing. People are dancing and swaying to the beats while again there are people up on the balcony throwing out beaded necklaces to the dancers below.

"Want to go in?" Andrew asks us. Zagreus and I look at each other.

"We aren't old enough." I tell him.

"Oh, don't even worry about that, I've got it covered. Let's go!" Before we know it, Andrew is walking up to the bouncer, we reluctantly follow him. "Hey man!" He says to the bouncer and before I even understand what is happening, Andrew stands directly in front of him and makes the guy look deeply into his eyes, "*Me and the two people behind me are all over twenty-one.*" Andrew tells him and the bouncer nods, pulling out three wristbands and placing them on each of our wrists.

"What just happened?" I ask.

"Man! I have been *dying* to try that!" Andrew exclaims, "And it worked! Can you believe it?" He pulls us into the bar behind him.

"Andrew you shouldn't have done that." Zagreus tells him, his voice is low.

"Oh, what's the harm?"

"It messes with people, Andrew." Zagreus growls.

"It's not any different than what you do when taking away people's memories Z. That guy will be fine." Andrew challenges. I feel useless as I watch them, neither one backing down until Zagreus waves his hand for Andrew to carry on. Andrew excuses himself to the bathroom while Zagreus and I hang back.

"What was that?" I ask him.

"Andrew compelled that man." Zagreus tells me.

"Compelled? What do you mean?" I ask.

"He made him believe what Andrew wanted him to believe, Aphrodite must have told him about more than she should have when I told her to train him."

"I mean, I know what compulsion is, it's like a staple in every vampire movie, but I didn't think it was real." I tell him, "But it could come in handy, couldn't it? If used for the right reason." I try to reason.

"No, it'll get us caught or worse *killed*. But it doesn't matter. What's done is done." Zagreus states, Andrew comes out of the bathroom dancing.

"Listen guys, I'm sorry. I won't do it again. let's just have fun tonight. That's all I was trying to do." Andrew says. I smile at him, and he grabs my wrist, "Yes! Rose gets it, Come on Z!" Andrew shakes my arm trying to get me to dance and slowly pulls me out onto the dance floor. Zagreus shakes his head, rolls his eyes, and follows us out onto the dance floor. We dance together for the rest of the song before Andrew finds someone else to dance with. I can't help but feel like something is different with him right now, but I push that feeling down. Maybe he's just feeling like a third wheel without Gabby here. I know I would if the roles were reversed.

The band transitions to a slower paced one and Zagreus holds out his hand for mine, "May I have this dance?" He asks, I smile and take his hand.

"Always." I tell him placing my arms around his neck and his places his hands firmly on my hips. We dance together to only the music for a minute, just staring at one another, I barely even worry about stepping on his feet.

"You really do look beautiful tonight." He tells me.

"Thank you," I blush. "I meant what I said earlier too."

"Are you doing alright?" He asks me and I smile.

"I've never been better, than I am in this moment." I wrap my arms around him tighter and hug him. "Thank you for this." I pull back and he checks his watch, five minutes until midnight.

"Want to go outside and get a better view of the fleur-de-lis drop?" He asks pulling away from me.

"For sure." I smile, take his hand and he leads us outside.

The crowd has grown thicker, if possible, but Zagreus and I manage to get a good spot next to the water where we can see the top of the building holding the fleur-de-lis. I don't let go of his hand, partly because I'm worried that if I do then we'll get separated, but mostly because I don't want to. It has been a long year, all of it leading up to this very moment. The lights reflect on the top of the water, painting a blurry image of the city around us. I want to remember everything about this moment, to be able to replay it in my brain for years to come. All the good things, all the bad, it all made me who I am. Maybe Medusa was right, I did have an unfair life. But it is my life, my choice. I have always been distant, and unavailable. Always kept my heart locked away, not out of strategy, but from fear. And fear has kept me safe, but it has also kept me from a lot of things. Fear has kept me from opening myself to people, from loving. Because a heart of stone doesn't need warmth, compassion, or care, it doesn't need anything.

The crowd begins to count-down from ten, Zagreus squeezes my hand, and we count down with them. *"Seven, six, five, four, three, two, one!"* we shout together, the fleur-de-lis sinks to the bottom of its' pole and sends fireworks shooting into the sky. Bright blue, red, and green sparks shoot into the dark sky and burst covering the crowd in bright lights. Without hesitation, Zagreus lifts my arm and twirls me around until I'm facing him, "Happy New Year, darling." He smiles, I squeeze his hand and pull him into me, wrapping my arms around his neck and I kiss him. It's like the world explodes in a world of color around us, and I can finally feel the warmth, my heart of stone crumbles and the fear disappears.

"Happy New Year, Zagreus." I whisper as I pull back and he smiles with his eyes still closed and his forehead resting on mine, then pulls me back in for another kiss.

We walk back to the bar hand in hand. This time not out of fear of losing the other to the crowd; but out of necessity, out of desire, and out of hope that this time, nothing would keep us apart.

I should have known something was wrong. Before we even stepped foot into the bar we should have just gone down to the waterfront and watched the fireworks together, the three of us. I should have turned around the second we decided to leave and made sure that Andrew came with us. Zagreus and I never should have left without Andrew.

"Zagreus." I grab his bicep and stop walking. "He isn't here." We have searched the entire building three times and still nothing. Still no Andrew.

"Where else could he be?" He says, still looking around the building.

"He could have gone back to the hotel."

"They said that the door hasn't been activated since we got back at sunset and nobody matching his description is anywhere in that hotel." He still hasn't given up looking around.

"Zagreus." I say, he doesn't look at me or even ac-knowledge me. "Zagreus!" I say louder and he finally looks at me. "I'm scared." I admit.

"It's alright, we will find him. I promise." He tells me, wrapping his arms around me and hugging me tightly. "Let's just check outside, Okay? The crowd has cleared a bit, maybe he's just watching one of the musicians or something." He offers and leads me out of the bar. I try to focus on Andrew, try to separate his voice out of the crowd or catch his scent but there is no trace of him; there is just too many people. Zagreus walks me to the sidewalk, "Stay here." He tells me and he walks back to the bouncer. "Did you see the guy we came in with? Did go somewhere?" He asks the bouncer. I watch them intently, but as the bouncer speaks a group of loud girls pass by me and I can't make out what he says. Zagreus comes back to me and grabs my hand. "Come on, he went this way." He pulls me in a direction, and I follow.

We walk through the crowds of people, zigzagging in and out of the way of street vendors and musicians. I can't believe there are still so many people out at this time of night, but I can't believe that Andrew ran off even more. We don't stop walking until we reach the water's edge and Zagreus stops to make sure I'm okay.

"I'm fine, but what did the bouncer say? Why do you look so worried." I ask him.

"He said that Andrew left with a group of people, and what direction they left in, but he couldn't tell me anything else." Zagreus says breathlessly, "But I need you to focus for me, can you do that?" He asks and I nod, "Good, I need you to try really hard to smell or maybe hear him."

"I already tried that." I groan.

"I know." He rubs my shoulders, "I know you did, but there's less people here, maybe you can catch something here." Something about the urgency in his voice worries me but I nod.

"Okay. Okay, just stop talking." I tell him and I close my eyes. At first, I don't hear or smell anything, just the water as it slaps against the earth. I focus harder, trying to replicate my bond with Phoenix like I had when he was locked in the school by Melinoe. The wind blows against my face, and I shiver, but then it hits me, and I smell him. I open my eyes; Zagreus is still staring intently at me. "The wind. The wind is carrying his scent. So, we should just go in that direction, right?" I ask him.

"Yes!" He grabs my face and kisses me quickly, "You are amazing! Let's go!" he grabs my hand again and we head in the direction that the wind is coming from. We move quickly, only slowing occasionally to make sure I can still smell Andrew, but his scent is getting stronger, and I know we are on the right track.

We follow Andrew's scent all the way up the water's edge to an aquarium. It is a large, white-tiled round building with big windows and palm trees lining the sidewalk, but all the lights inside are off and there isn't any sign of anyone being around. It's like a ghost town outside and the temperature seems to be dropping every minute.

"Can you still smell him?" Zagreus asks.

"Yeah, like he was just here seconds ago."

"Then he has to be around here somewhere, come on." We walk around the building, looking for any sign that Andrew is here, until we come up to a side door that is propped open with a rock. I peak my head in the doorway and take a breath.

"He's inside." I tell Zagreus.

"Why would he come to an aquarium?" Zagreus asks, I don't answer him, but he doesn't seem to notice. "I guess we'll find out then."

"Zagreus wait." I grab his arm as he starts towards the door.

"What?"

"He isn't alone." I tell him.

"I mean the bouncer said he left with some people, so I figured." He starts towards the door again, but I squeeze his arm tighter, holding him back.

"When I was smelling for Andrew, I was able to focus on his smell because he still smells like the cows' blood from the underworld." I begin telling him, "But now that we are here, I don't think it is cows' blood that I'm smelling." Zagreus gives me a worried look before looking back at the door.

"Rose, stay behind me. We *need* to get him out of here before it's too late." He tells me.

"Too late for what?" I ask him, but he shakes his head.

"We really don't have time for answers, I promise I will tell you everything when we get through this. Just trust me." He urges.

"Okay," I nod. "I trust you."

4

Dead Man Walking

I have never been to an aquarium, and as we walk through the barely lit tunnel-like corridors, I don't think I ever want to. The hallway is barely lit, with only every other box light turned on and it smells like a hospital. Occasionally we pass by signs for the numerous fish, and I pray that we don't find Andrew floating in a shark tank. I follow closely behind Zagreus as we make our way through the twists and turns of the building, trying to hear Andrews or anyone's voice over the loud humming of the fish tanks and generators.

"Zagreus, hang on a second." I tell him and he stops.

"What, do you hear something?" He asks, I grab his shoulder.

"No, I can't hear anything over the sound of these heels." I lift my leg and use Zagreus' shoulder for balance as I undo the straps of my heels; I knew I would regret wearing these. I struggle for a moment before he grabs my arm.

"Here, let me help." He bends down and starts working on the strap, he gets them off my feet in less than thirty seconds.

"I loosened it." I glare at him, and he chuckles at me, "Okay but seriously, how did you do that so fast?"

"Let's just say that there's a reason I'm glad that gladiator sandals never made a comeback." He winks at me, "Now wipe that smirk off your face and let's keep going." He hands me my shoes and I try to wipe the image of him in gladiator sandals from my mind.

As we approach a door at the end of the corridor, I start to hear voices. Zagreus turns to face me and holds a finger up to his mouth, telling me to be quiet. It sounds like multiple conversations are happening because I can't make out a single sentence from behind the door. But what I can make out is bottles clinking together and cheering, then silence before a single voice speaks out louder above the others.

"Looks like we have company friends!" the voice calls out, "let's see who is behind door number one, shall we?" Footsteps approach from the other side of the door before Zagreus throws it open, knocking someone back as he does so. There is so much movement that I don't know where to look. Two figures shake the rafters above us, another two move quickly around the lobby desk in the middle of the room, one stands on the desk and another one sits on the chair behind it. My eyes dart to each of them, searching for Andrew, but I don't see him. I follow Zagreus into the room, letting the door swing closed behind me. He stands tall in front of me, not allowing me to stand beside him.

"We came for our friend." Zagreus announces to the room.

The man in the desk chair laughs and stands up, "We are all friends here. You're going to have to be more specific." He speaks clearly, like he is used to commanding a room. He is tall, not as tall as Zagreus or Andrew, but taller than me, with close-cropped, platinum blonde hair and pearl-white skin. He looks familiar to me for some reason, but I brush it off.

"Andrew." Zagreus says.

The man clicks his tongue, "Ah, the young one. Very well, bring him out." He waves his hand at the man who is standing on the desk, but he doesn't move. "Did you not hear me, Cal?" he turns to face the man he is speaking to. "I said, *bring him out.*" He says again, the desk walker—Cal, jumps down and goes behind the desk and through the 'employee's only' door and a moment later, He and a girl with dark hair and the same pearl-white skin as the others, walk out with Andrew behind them. I move towards Andrew, but Zagreus blocks me.

"Hey guys, what're you doing here?" Andrew asks sloppily, he sounds drunk to me, and his shirt is no longer tucked in, it's wrinkled and there is no sign of the jacket he was wearing earlier.

"It's time to go Andrew." Zagreus tells him, his jaw is tight, along with all the other muscles in his body.

"Oh, but the young vampire doesn't want to go." The man replies for him, "Do you Drew?" My skin crawls as he speaks.

"No, guys. Hang out with us for a while. They're a lot of fun. You'll like them." I can barely make out what Andrew is saying, he doesn't even sound like himself right now. The man smirks as Andrew speaks and I want to hit them both.

"Andrew, it's late. And we should really get you back to the hotel before sunrise." I speak up.

Andrew squints at me like he can hardly see me, "No, Rosey, it's okay. These guys are vampires too, they said I'll be okay with them." I swallow, trying to bury the fear I'm feeling deep down. I didn't know there were other vampires. I mean sure, they had to exist, but I didn't think they would be here. I didn't think we would ever meet another one.

"I understand, but it's been a long night already. Don't you want to get some rest?" I offer.

"Oh, come now, why the rush? We should really get to know each other better. I presume this is the god and the wolf you mentioned earlier, youngblood." The man speaks, I can see Zagreus's nostrils flare. I'm not sure if I've ever seen him this angry. The man walks closer to us, "Tell me then, what is your name dear?" He addresses me, Zagreus moves more in front of me slightly.

"Rose." I answer him, Zagreus looks back at me like he is warning me to keep my mouth shut.

"Such a fitting name for such a beautiful woman." The man states, looking directly at Zagreus. "I am Cyrus, thank you for asking." He smirks darkly as he turns to each of his 'friends' and points, "You've met Cal, the woman next to him is his sister, Gwen, the two that were up on the rafters are Axel and Lucas, and the two at either end of the desk are Marcus and Devon." Cyrus tells us, "And you," He points to Zagreus, "Must be the son of Hades, Zagreus." He says his name by emphasizing the z sound. "Now that we are all acquainted, why don't you stay a while, join in on the festivities, it is a New Year after all." His eyes glisten in the harsh lighting around us. Zagreus doesn't move, instead he maintains eye contact with Cyrus, who is clearly the leader of this vampire group. Andrew sways back and forth as if he is listening to music none of us can hear, I want to grab him and run like hell out of here, but my instincts tell me that if I move any closer, I won't make it two feet. "Why don't you join us for a midnight snack?" Cyrus asks, "We were just about to enjoy ourselves a tasty security guard." As he says this, Gwen kicks the other chair behind the desk and spins it around to reveal a middle-aged man passed out with his hands tied. I can't help but take a step forward, but Zagreus pushes me back. The vampires all move forward too but they stop when Cyrus snaps his fingers. "That wasn't very polite friends, the poor girl just wants to *save* the poor man." They all laugh like hyenas; it echoes throughout the room.

"You know what will happen if Andrew drinks from him." Zagreus says through gritted teeth.

"Do I?" Cyrus asks, crossing his arms and tapping his foot, "I'm not sure I do. Maybe you should tell us."

Zagreus is breathing heavily; I can see the vein on his temple. He is thinking hard about what he is going to say, but I'm not sure why. "He will never be human again." He states, but I don't understand.

"The girl looks confused, why don't you clarify?" Cyrus smirks. I look at Zagreus, but he doesn't say anything. "Well, if he won't, I will." He rounds the desk, walking slowly up to the security guard. And placing a hand on his shoulder. "You see, Rose, vampires were an accident, created by multiple gods. I'm sure you were told the story of Ambrosio, a man so love-stricken by our mother Selene that he would do anything to remain with her, thus leading him on the path to becoming the first vampire. I will spare you the details for the sake of time. But there is a test, one that the gods don't like to talk about. We vampires require a steady supply of blood to get us by, and while the blood of an animal certainly can curb the craving, it does not fully satiate them. Only the blood of another human can do such a thing. Now, when a vampire gives in to these *cravings,* he—" Cyrus turns to Gwen, "or she," he turns back and makes direct eye contact with me. "Eliminates any chance of ever becoming human again. But if the vampire can overcome these cravings, by the first full moon of the new year they will be visited by the mother of all vampires and given the choice between remaining a vampire or going back to the life of a human." Cyrus smiles, "But of course, these are all rumors. We have never met a vampire able to make the sacrifice."

"Is he..." I breathe, "Is he telling the truth, Zagreus?" I ask but he doesn't say anything, and he doesn't look at me either, instead he maintains whatever masculine power pose he has going on.

"Of course, I speak the truth. What reason would I have to lie to you, beautiful." Cyrus sneers. I find myself torn between feeling betrayed and feeling terrified of how dangerously close Cyrus is to the security guard. "Poor girl, look at the betrayal on her face." He fake pouts, before coming back around the desk, moving closer to us. "Is this what you want gorgeous? To be like Persephone? Loved tenderly by a god, to lay claim to his power and his kingdom. We have all heard *that* story before. Don't be such an Icarus, dear, for he will only throw you to the sea in the end. Broken and burned, left for dead without so much as a care." He scoffs, "You think he cares for you? He couldn't even tell you the truth. Join us and let me show you how a real man loves a woman." He holds out his hand to me with a smug smirk on his face. I take a moment to observe the room, Cyrus is the closest to us, Andrew is behind him with Cal to his left and Gwen has taken Cyrus' spot next to the security guard, Marcus and Devon haven't moved since we got here and the other two, Axel and Lucas are still up in the rafters looking down on us. It is only this moment that I realize Cyrus forgot to introduce us to the vampire that Zagreus knocked over with the door and I feel his presence behind us, blocking the way we came. I don't know what to do. I weigh my options in my head, I don't know how much Andrew has told them. I don't know if he underestimates me, but he knows I'm a wolf. He must be trying to trick me, what could he possibly want with me other than to kill me or get to Zagreus to kill him. I can't even imagine what is running through his mind.

I take a deep breath and step forward, dropping the heels from my hand. Zagreus looks at me but doesn't move as I take another step forward and take Cyrus's hand. Cyrus' grin grows wider, my heart feels like it is going to beat itself out of my chest. I look back at Zagreus, "Trust me," I mouth, and he doesn't react at all. Cyrus leads me farther away from Zagreus and closer to Andrew, then with a quick pull, Cyrus drags me into him. Zagreus takes a step toward us, but the vampire behind him gets right up to his back.

"Just, please don't hurt her." Zagreus pleads.

"Hurt her? No, I would never," Cyrus sneers, and brushes the hair away from my face. "I'm just going to play with her. Show her how powerful I can be." His eyes narrow and he squeezes my hand.

"You want to talk about power?" I whisper to him, biting my lip "Let me show *you* power." I twist his wrist and push him back, drop to the floor and kick Andrews' feet out from under him causing him to hit the ground as Cal lunges for him but misses, tripping over his body and hitting the far wall trying to regain his balance. The other vampires begin to react, but I am already in motion. I kick the security guards chair back, knocking Gwen into the wall behind them. Zagreus grabs the arm of the vampire behind him and flips him over his body, dropping him to the floor before moving onto the two vampires that dropped from the rafters. I duck a punch from Marcus that causes him to punch Devon and distracts them both long enough for me to turn into a wolf and lunge for Cyrus again. I hit him square in the chest, sending us both to the ground but I remain on top of him, pinning him to the ground with my paws.

"Enough!" Cyrus bellows. All the vampires stop moving, aside from Andrew who groggily begins to rise from the floor. "Let them go." Cyrus commands making eye contact with me. I slowly back off him, reverting to a human as I do so.

"We are taking Andrew with us." I tell him.

"But of course." He hisses and narrows his eyes. I move to Andrew and grab his arm, pulling him towards Zagreus. Cal moves to help Cyrus from the floor. Zagreus grabs Andrews' other arm and I scoop up my heels as we lead him to the door we came in from. When we reach the door, I look back to see Cyrus wiping his clothes off and the security guard still tied to the chair.

"He's already dead." Zagreus tells me, throwing the door open and ushering us through.

As the door is about to click shut behind us, I hear Cyrus one last time, "Get them." He spits.

"We need to get out of here," I tell the boys, and Zagreus and I quicken our pace down the hallway.

"Rose, we need a plan." Zagreus tells me.

"This was the plan." I grunt as I try to keep Andrew balanced next to me. Behind us, the vampire's footsteps grow closer, faster than I could have anticipated; I wish we would have barricaded the door behind us. The lights overhead flicker, and while part of me can't help but picture one of them messing with the light-switch, my horror film knowledge tells me to leave everyone behind before the ghost faced killer sticks a knife in my back. We make it about halfway down the hallway before it sounds like the footsteps are right on top of us.

"Take him and go." Zagreus shifts more of Andrews weight onto me, "I mean it, keep going and don't come back. I will meet back up with you when I can." He says and then he is gone and I'm carrying Andrew alone. Thankfully, Andrew has regained some of his composure and is able to speed up, if we make it out of this alive, I'm going to kill him. Ignoring the smacks and grunting that I hear behind us, we reach the door at the end of the hall.

The cold air hits me in the face sharply as we stumble outside, and the door slams shut behind us. I drop Andrew next to one of the palm trees and catch my breath.

"I swear to god if you move an inch, I will hurt you." I threaten him and turn back to help Zagreus but as I do so, it looks like all the electricity in the building surges. A light so bright builds, escaping through every crack in the building that it can until the lights in the building burst, sending sparks flying in every direction. I run back to the door, only for Zagreus to come out coughing as I get there.

Zagreus grabs for me and I pull him into me, "I told you to keep going." He wheezes.

"I couldn't leave you behind." I tell him, hugging him tighter.

"Of course, you couldn't." He almost laughs but it turns into another cough, he runs his hands through my hair and kisses the side of my head.

"Did you stop them?" I ask him.

"For now, but we need to get back to the hotel. They won't be able to come after us tonight, so we leave as soon as possible." He pulls away from me but drapes his arm around my shoulders as we make or way over to Andrew, who thankfully, hasn't moved an inch.

"What the hell were you thinking!" I yell at him; Andrew closes his eyes and shakes his head.

"I wasn't." He speaks.

"We could have died because of you!" I tell him.

"I know. I was reckless, I was stupid." He rubs his temple, "I'm sorry." He takes a deep breath and lets it out slowly, "It was like I wasn't in control of myself, like I was separated from my body, watching it from above and unable to stop myself from doing anything."

"That's what happens when you get drunk." I tell him but he shakes his head.

"No, this was something different." He sighs, "I was still me, but like not. Does that make sense?"

"No." I say flatly.

"Actually, it does." Zagreus states. "But we should really get moving, we can talk back at the hotel." He reaches out to help Andrew up from the ground. "Are you okay to walk by yourself?" He asks him.

"Yeah, I think I can manage." Andrew answers. Zagreus reaches for my hand, and I gladly take it, he seems to have recovered from whatever happened back in the corridor of the aquarium. "Glad to see you two have warmed up to each other again." Andrew chuckles and I fight the urge to trip him.

The amount of people still partying on the streets is shocking. As we make our way back to the hotel, they seem to be coming from nowhere in particular; a stark contrast to the aquarium where it felt like a ghost-town. Zagreus forced me to put my heels back on, it was either that or he was going to carry me the whole way back because he didn't want to risk my foot getting cut on broken glass or something and I wasn't about to piggy-back for an entire mile. But he did give me his jacket to wear, so that was nice. Andrew at this point seems to be feeling better, he drags his feet a little bit, but that's just something he has always done. The walk back to the hotel reminds me of the million-step staircase to the underworld, the three of us walking slowly, not talking, and wondering what on earth could possibly go wrong next.

When we walk into the hotel room, the three of us collapse on the couch together, Zagreus, Me, and Andrew. I'm not sure which, but one of the boys turns the tv on cross from us. A local news recap of the Fleur-de-lis drop is on. The three of us erupt in laughter, whether its form exhaustion or what I'm not sure. Somewhere on the counter in the kitchen a phone begins vibrating.

"Not mine." Zagreus says.

"Mine either." Andrew shakes his head.

"You really lost the jacket Medusa gave to you as a gift, but you managed to hold onto your phone?" I make fun of him. Zagreus gets up and looks at the phone.

"Rose, it's yours." He says and he tosses the phone over to me.

"Mine?" I catch it and look at the screen. I shrug out of Zagreus's jacket, stand up and answer it, "Deme?" the other line is quiet. "Deme? Are you there? Are you okay?"

"Rose." Demes' voice squeaks out from the speaker. *It's her, it's really her!* Andrew mutes the television.

"Deme! Oh, I miss you so much, is everything okay? How are you?" I ask her.

"Listen." She says, "Andrew is in trouble. Other. Vampires. Danger." She speaks slowly, as if she is thinking hard about the words that she is saying.

"No, it's okay. We got him, he is safe. Deme, please, are you okay?" The boys are staring at me intently, but Deme doesn't answer me, instead I hear a shuffling sound from the other line.

"Who is this?" My father's voice barks through the receiver.

"Dad it's me." I sigh.

"Rose? What happened, is everything alright?" He sounds concerned.

"Everything is fine Dad, we got to Andrew in time. It's all okay. How are you guys?" I explain.

"Got to Andrew in time? What does that mean?" He asks, avoiding my question.

"It was nothing okay, how is Deme, how are you? What is going on over there?" I urge.

"We're okay, everything is quiet here. Your sister is getting treatment, and it is going well for now, but she shouldn't have distractions like this." My dad explains.

"She called me." I tell him.

"She did? Well, she shouldn't have. Hang on a moment will ya?" I hear footsteps and a door shut, "Are you still there, Rose?"

"Yeah, I'm still here." I answer.

"I'm sorry for being short with you, but it's been difficult until now and I don't want anything happening that could send her backwards."

"I understand."

"Thank you." He sighs, "Have you talked to your brother?"

"No, not since..." I trail off.

"I thought so." We are both quiet for a minute. "I should get back to your sister."

"Okay Dad. I love you." I tell him.

"Love you too kiddo." He says, "Oh and Rose?"

"Yeah?"

"Stay safe out there."

"I will." I tell him.

We say our goodbyes and I hang up the phone. It feels like it has been years since I last heard their voices, I begin to tear up.

"Are they okay?" Andrew asks.

"Yeah," my voice cracks and I compose myself. "Yeah, they are okay." Zagreus reaches out and takes the phone from my hand, places it on the table and leads me back to the couch with him. He wraps his arm around my shoulders and pulls me in close to him as we sit down next to Andrew.

"What did Deme say?" Andrew asks me.

"She basically said there were other vampires and that you were in trouble." I tell him, Andrew scrunches his nose up. "Yeah, don't think you got out of that one so easily." I warn him.

"I said I was sorry."

"You *were* sorry, or you *are* sorry?" I tilt my head and smile.

"I am sorry." He clarifies and hits me with one of the couch pillows.

"Was Cyrus telling the truth?" I look up at Zagreus, I can tell by the look on his face that he has been dreading this question.

"Yes." He states.

"Then why didn't you tell us that there was a cure." I ask.

"Because it has only happened once. Cyrus was right, most vampires aren't strong enough to remain off human blood for that long." Zagreus rubs his eyebrows with his thumb and index finger. "I was hoping we could keep Andrew locked up and hidden away long enough that he wouldn't experience what it was really like to be a vampire and he would be cured. I wasn't expecting anything like tonight to ever happen." He explains.

"So, you really were keeping me prisoner." Andrew says, I pinch his arm.

"That's not what he meant." I tell him.

"But that's what Cyrus called it." Andrew rubs his arm and glares at me. "He told me you were keeping me prisoner, and that I needed to be with my own kind."

"Is that why you went with him?"

"Yes and no. Like I said, I wasn't entirely in control."

"When someone becomes a vampire, they become the best version of themselves." Zagreus tells us, "Your personalities have been battling it out since you were turned, fighting to decide which would become your dominant one. It makes sense that you went with them." Zagreus rubs my shoulder with his finger, drawing patterns on my skin as he talks, "You've always been outgoing, and have always been a little more spontaneous than Rose and me. That is the personality that is taking over. You didn't think twice about going with them because you have always just handled the things life threw at you rather than worry about the outcomes of these situations." He explains.

"I guess that makes sense." I respond.

"And because you are a vampire now, you might feel like you don't need to worry about things going wrong because you are more powerful than a human now. You have senses they don't, can lift ten times the amount they can and move faster too."

"But Rose's senses are heightened too, and she isn't just running off all willy-nilly." Andrew says and we're all quiet for a moment, "Actually wait, I take that back. She did run off to go find Medusa by herself."

"And went to take on my sister by herself before that." Zagreus adds.

"And tried to fight the Vry by herself too." Andrew smiles.

"And fought the—" Zagreus starts but I cut him off.

"Okay, okay, when did this become about me?" I fight back, they both laugh.

"I'm only saying, you *both* need to be more careful out there. Just because you have the power to back up your words, doesn't mean you need to use it, nor should you rely on it either. You guys haven't had your abilities long enough." Zagreus explains, I raise my eyebrow at him, and he winks at me, I try not to melt in his arms.

"What was that thing that you did though?" Andrew asks.

"What thing?" Zagreus asks him to clarify.

"The thing with the lights back at the aquarium." He answers.

"Oh, that." Zagreus sits up a little, "That was me channeling a lot of power and scorching the skin of the vampires enough that they couldn't follow us anymore." He states.

"Is that why you were coughing? Because it took so much out of you?" I tease.

"Me? No, I can actually handle the power I wield. I was coughing because the smell of cooked flesh is disgusting." Zagreus states smugly, I fake gag.

"But they'll just heal themselves, right?" Andrew asks.

"Yeah, but it'll take time. I don't think this will be the last time we see Cyrus though, we should leave town, so we have a head start on them." Zagreus answers.

"It wasn't the first time I'd seen him." I admit to them.

"Then they were on to us before we even knew they existed." Zagreus leans his head back, looking up at the ceiling. "We should get some rest then, and head out in a few hours. The jeep is parked in the underground lot, so Andrew can take the elevator straight down to avoid the sunlight."

"Sounds good to me." Andrew yawns and stretches his arms out widely, pushing me closer to Zagreus, "I'm going to bed then." He stands up and winks at me, "Goodni-ight!" He sings and heads into his room, closing the door behind him with a soft *click*.

"You should go to bed too," Zagreus speaks quietly in my ear and twirls a strand of my hair in his fingers. I close my eyes and breathe deeply. Zagreus chuckles and starts to get up. "Come on." He pulls me up and leads me to my room.

I sit on the bed while Zagreus undoes the straps of my heels for me again. When they're off, he places them neatly in the box they came in. I wiggle my now free toes and stretch my feet before grabbing a t-shirt and a pair of sleep shorts. "Can you get my zipper?" I ask him on my way to the bathroom. He comes up behind me and pulls it down while I hold the front of the dress up, when he's done with the zipper, he kisses my shoulder lightly. I don't want him to stop, but he lightly pushes me towards the bathroom, and I relent, closing the door behind me to change. I strip the dress from my body, stepping out of the skirt and putting it back on the hanger, I then wipe the remaining makeup from my face, brush my teeth, and hair, and get redressed into the shirt and shorts.

Zagreus is sitting on the bed when I come out of the bathroom. He stands and pulls the blankets back before patting the bed to call me over. I slip into bed, and he pulls the blankets over me, moves a piece of hair from my face, tucking it behind my ear and kisses my forehead, "Goodnight, Rose." He whispers and starts to pull away, but I grab his hand to stop him.

"Don't go." I say quietly and lock eyes with him. "Stay with me tonight, you deserve to sleep in a bed too." I add. I can tell he wants to; I can see the gears turning in his head, but he doesn't say anything. "Please?" I whisper.

"Okay. But just to sleep." He relents and I drop his hand. "I'll be right back." He goes out the door and comes back a moment later with his bag and takes it into the bathroom with him before shutting the door; I hear the shower start. I roll over, close my eyes, and take a deep breath. Medusa's words clinging to my mind.

You must choose him if that is what you want. The boy will wait for you till the end if he must.

Zagreus opens the bathroom door and I turn my head to look at him. He has changed into black pajama bottoms and his shirt is off. He wipes his head with a towel and shakes his hair back and forth before hanging the towel to dry. He hits the light switch in the bathroom, walks to the one by the bedroom door and flicks it, turning off the overhead light, but the table lamps on either side of the bed are on a manual switch so they stay on. Zagreus pulls the blankets back and gets in bed, his muscles flex as he reaches up and turns the lamp off next to him. When he turns back and faces me, it takes every bit of willpower I have, to not kiss him. I start to reach for the lamp on my own table when he stops me, "I'll get it." He says, reaching over me. Does he know what he's doing to me? He must, otherwise he wouldn't be doing it. Right? He is stretched over me, and when he turns the light out for a fleeting moment, he doesn't move.

I expected his kiss, it was right there, waiting hungrily between us. I didn't expect his hands as one tightens around my waist and the other caresses my jawline. I didn't expect my own hands, one tracing his spine, the other in his damp hair, pulling him closer to me. Obediently listening to my body, he kisses my neck. This time, it takes everything I have not to wrap my legs around him. The city lights reflect along the ceiling, leaving intricate shadows around the room. I let out a soft, involuntary sigh, and his lips return to mine, his hand on my waist carefully rising to just below my ribcage. This isn't a soft kiss—not slow, nor explorative. It is fire, burning and longing for more, and not just on my part.

"Rose," he says my name so quietly, I can feel his regret in the words he hasn't even spoken yet. Zagreus breathes, suddenly pulling back. My lips are still warm from his kiss; my waist on fire where he touched my skin. "I... there's..." He trails off, opening his eyes and looking at me. "There is something I need to tell you."

"I already know." I whisper.

"You know?" his brow furrows.

"And I..." I sit up, bringing my face closer to his as he towers over me, "I choose you." I smile, "I choose you, and only you."

"Do you even know what you are saying right now?" He asks, his eyes so focused on mine, as if studying them for answers.

"I love you, Zagreus." I tell him, the words falling effortlessly from my lips. "I love you," I say again, "you awaken something inside of me that I have never felt before, and I don't ever want to be without you, I don't want to know a world without you in it. Always and forever, I love you." Zagreus leans back on his knees and takes my hands in his.

"I love you too, Rose." He lets out a sigh, like he has been holding in these words his entire life. He leans forward and kisses me, this time with a passion unlike any I have ever experienced. It sends chills down my spine and a fire that burns my bones. He pulls away slowly and rests his forehead on mine, the tips of our noses barely touching. "Now I'm never letting you go." He smiles.

Dead on the Beach

The drive to South Carolina is ten hours from New Orleans and we've been driving the entire day to get there. Only stopping for fuel and bathroom breaks. The sky is dark, the clouds pouring thick cold drops of rain onto the road ahead of us. I have never seen this much rain; it is almost impossible to see out of the windshield and the wipers are going full blast. We even had to stop once because it was too hard to see. If I hadn't checked the weather app numerous times beforehand, I would have thought we were driving in the middle of a hurricane. But as we get closer to our destination, the rain begins to slow, and I can make out the signs and buildings we pass by.

The homes we pass by are vibrant, shades of blue, yellow, pink, and green, all with their own personalities. The trees are plentiful, with Spanish moss that hangs over the limbs. We've been in so many cities lately that I almost forgot what a small town looks like, and I can't help but want to get out of the car and run through the wilderness. Zagreus squeezes my hand like he knows I want this.

Instead of finding a hotel, Zagreus drives us straight to the first bar that pops up on the map. Unfortunately, thanks to the one-hour time difference between New Orleans and South Carolina, it is closed. Zagreus parks the jeep in the dirt lot and stretches, "Want to get out and look around?" He asks turning the car off. We all get out and stretch our legs.

"What now?" Andrew asks groggily.

"We wait until its open I guess." Zagreus walks over and puts his arms around me.

"Do you really think this is the place?" I ask him.

"I mean, it's the closest to the ocean." He shrugs.

"We are on a literal island." Andrew states flatly, "we are surrounded by ocean."

"Maybe we should check out the boats over there." I point to the wooden dock where rows of different types of boats float along the bumpy waters. Andrew shrugs and we walk over to the dock.

The salty air tickles my nose as we walk across the wooden planks. The boats creak as we pass them, and flags slap in the wind. Andrew pulls his jacket tighter across his chest, and I use my pockets to keep my hands warm. Zagreus, who walks ahead of Andrew and I, stops to look at each boat before stopping at one and waving us over. We catch up with him and he points at the name painted delicately on the side THE AMPHRITE.

"That's Poseidon's wife's name." Zagreus tells us. I look around the boat, it doesn't look any different than the others in the marina. I mean, it looks a lot like the toy boat Deme, and I used to play dolls with, only this one is white and blue instead of bright pink. It has an enclosed cabin, with a steep staircase that leads up on top of the enclosed cabin, but I can't see what is up there. The boat bobs over the waves, occasionally revealing a stray barnacle attached to the side. As we get closer to the back of the boat, I notice there are a lot of nets and rope scattered around messily, and colorful fishing rods stick straight up from their holders, their bobbers drifting back and forth in the wind.

Zagreus steps up onto the back of the boat and looks around, "I can't tell if someone is here." He calls over to us as the cabin door slams open, and a large man bursts from the doorway holding a hooked knife to Zagreus' throat. I jump back, grabbing Andrew's arm, Zagreus doesn't move an inch.

"You just stepped foot on the wrong vessel, lad." The man growls. His hair is sandy blond, shorter on the sides of his head and slicked back on top with some kind of oil, and well-kept beard that covers his neck. He is wearing a white long-sleeved textured shirt, brown suspenders attached to his brown pants and a gold chain that sticks out of his pocket. What I thought was dirt or something on his face turns out to be a tattoo on his cheek of the tip of a trident just under his left eye.

"Poseidon." Zagreus says what I've only just figured out, and the man's brow furrows, his eyes squinting as he takes a closer look at Zagreus.

"You shouldn't be 'ere." The man tells him, lowering the knife.

"So, it's true," I say, "You're Poseidon."

He looks at me and squints again, "Don't speak that name so loudly, the sirens'll 'ear yah." He grunts at me, his accent I'd thick. He turns back to the cabin and goes inside. The three of us just look at each other. "Are ye comin' or not?" He calls from inside. Zagreus holds out his hand to help Andrew and I up on board and we follow Poseidon into the cabin.

The interior of the boat is much more luxurious than I thought it would be. There is a small kitchen, with a propane stove, microwave, and mini fridge. A rounded couch that reminds me of a restaurant booth, and folding table and in the corner on the right-hand side where Poseidon sits, is a steering wheel and more buttons, levers, and meters than I anticipated. Poseidon waves his hand at the booth-couch, and we all sit down. He rolls his sleeves up to reveal that his arms are covered in tattoos, each one covered in intricate designs ranging from mermaids and anchors to flowers and other sea creatures.

"How'd you find me?" He growls, leaning back in the seat sideways, one arm on the wheel and the other on the back of the chair. I can't help but notice that his accent is almost completely gone, now he speaks clearly, a lot like Ares does.

"Medusa." Zagreus answers him.

Poseidon scoffs, "leave it to a gorgon to blubber their mouth to the first one that'll listen." He grabs a bottle, drinks from it, and wipes his mouth with his sleeve. "What do you want?" He barks.

"Ares is—" Zagreus starts.

"That *fool*. I should've known. What is he up to now?"

"You don't know?" I ask him, although I regret opening my mouth immediately because the look that he gives me makes me feel like I could die.

"Haven't troubled myself with the mere thought of that idiot in years. But if you're 'ere, someone must've broke the rules." The three of us sit uncomfortably silent and Poseidon laughs, "Let me guess, it was you three." He points at us with the bottle in his hand and clicks his tongue three times. "And you want my help stopping the dumb kid." I can't help but notice that Poseidon never says Ares' name when referring to him. "What are two mortals and the son of Hades going to offer me in return for my help?" He asks, raising his scarred eyebrow.

"Werewolf." I raise my hand.

"Vampire." Andrew mumbles, Poseidon breaks out in a roaring laughter causing the entire boat to shake.

"I stand corrected." He takes another drink from the bottle. He slams the bottle down on the counter next to him, I jump in my seat and a wave rocks the boat. "Sounds like the beginning of a bad joke." He chuckles to himself. "So then, what are a god, a vampire and a werewolf going to offer me?"

"What do you want?" Zagreus asks him and the smile on Poseidon's face evaporates. He leans forward until he is barely sitting in his seat, and I can smell the sea salt on his skin.

"My *trident*." Poseidon states through his teeth.

"You're trident?" Zagreus sounds shocked.

"Yes, I would like you to retrieve my trident." Poseidon sits back in his seat smugly.

"But you cast the trident away, when Amphrite agreed to marry you." Zagreus starts.

"WRONG!" Poseidon yells, "I simply hid it from her." he adds. "Tell me why I would cast away my most prized possession for a woman?" He rolls his eyes, and I can't help but roll my own. "I've known exactly where it has been this entire time, until that siren got her grubby hands on it." He explains and grabs the bottle again.

"Siren." Zagreus repeats.

"I followed her to this island, but considering our little deal with that incompetent man-child, finding her has proved difficult." He spits.

"So that's it. We find the siren, bring back the trident and you'll help us." Andrew clarifies.

Poseidon lifts his eyebrows at him and nods, "Yes, I will assist where I am able, bloodsucker." He chuckles, clearly proud of himself. "Now get off my ship, I have things to do."

"How are we supposed to find someone, when we know absolutely nothing about them?" I ask, spreading jelly on a piece of toast. After our meeting with Poseidon, Zagreus drove us to a twenty-four-hour diner. The coffee is bitter and the air smells musty but it's a lot better than being shoved in the jeep figuring this out, and since the clouds are so thick from the storm, Andrew is able to be out in the daylight.

"Isn't a siren the same thing as a mermaid?" Andrew asks through mouthfuls of eggs and hashbrowns.

"No." Zagreus frowns at him. "Sirens are dangerous, and mermaids are not. A siren can lure you in with a song and kill you before you would think to cover your ears. Mermaids are mostly there for you to look at."

I raise my eyebrow at him. "Excuse me?" I ask, Zagreus chokes on his bacon.

"Sorry," He mutters when he collects himself. "I just meant that they aren't anything special."

"That better be what you meant." I mumble under my breath.

"So, sirens sing, and they like water." Andrew says, "Shouldn't we just go to the beach and look for one of those street performers?"

"Not if she really has the trident." Zagreus tells him, "The trident is almost as dangers as Zeus's thunderbolt. It can kill you without the carrier trying, cause hurricanes and cyclones. If a siren really has it, she would be on land, otherwise Poseidon would have found her already."

"So, sirens like singing." Andrew amends his earlier statement.

"We've been told, how does that help us exactly?" I ask him.

"Well, I don't know about you, but if I liked singing, I'd probably try my hand at some karaoke." Andrew takes another bite of his eggs. Zagreus and I just look at each other. "There's a flyer on the bulletin board behind you." He points with his butterknife without even looking up from his plate.

"Are you seeing what I'm seeing?" I ask.

"You've got to be kidding." Zagreus answers.

"Mermaids Grotto: Bar and Grill." Andrew reads, "Pretty obvious if you ask me."

Since we have an entire day to kill, we find a hotel down the road and book a room. It is a *serious* downgrade from the hotel in New Orleans, but it still has charm. The room has two beds, each with a giant black and white photo of scenery from the area, and the walls are painted vibrant colors. Andrew sprawls out over one of the beds and belches. I drop my bag on the table and look out the window. I can't help but wonder what Deme is doing right now. I pull my phone out and look at the time, its nearly noon which means that in Greece it is around seven o'clock.

"Hey guys, I'm gonna step out for a second." I tell the boys, and they nod before I slip out of the hotel door, out into the fresh air. I dial Deme's number and press send, hoping this is a good time to call. She answers on the third ring.

"Rose!" Deme sounds good, like she used to.

"Hey! How are you? It has been a while since I was able to talk to you." I say, sitting down on a log that is being used to mark a parking space. "Is this a good time?" I ask.

"Yeah, its perfect!" She tells me, "I'm doing better, it's a little boring here to be honest."

"Boring? What do you mean? You guys are in one of the most beautiful places, how could you be bored?"

She sighs, "Hold on, lets switch to a video call." Deme presses a button and my phone rings for a second before I accept the video request. She looks ten times better than the last time I saw her; it feels like months since the last time instead of weeks. Her face is a little thinner, but she looks older, her tanned skin is clearer and her dark auburn hair that used to be a bob is now grown past her shoulders.

"Wow, you look amazing. The sun must be doing wonders for your skin." I tell her.

"I wish, we don't really have time to go out as much as I'd like to." She sighs again.

"Why not?"

"Dad had me pretty much on lockdown when we first got here. I wasn't allowed to leave the room until he tracked down that oracle lady and even then, I didn't really get to leave her house." She explains. In the background I can see that the windows are all covered in white curtains that let little sunlight through. "But enough about me, tell me everything! I want to know what's been going on since we last saw each other."

"Where do I even start?" I laugh thinking back over all of the things we've seen and the places we've been. "Well, you know that Andrew was kidnapped by vampires, right?"

"Yes, that was by far the scariest vision I've had since we got here. That blond vampire was so *creepy*" she shudders at the thought.

"Yeah, that was really intense, but before that I got to meet Medusa." I tell her.

"Wait," Her eyes widen, "Like Medusa, *the* Medusa." She makes gestures around her head like snakes. "She's real?"

"Yeah, super real." I smile, "At first I was terrified, but talking to her was so easy, almost as easy as talking to you."

"What did you guys talk about?" Deme asks, the phone shifts slightly as she gets comfortable in her chair.

"We talked about everything, I mean once I started talking, I couldn't stop, almost like I was under a spell or something, but she just listened, and it was really nice to talk to someone who didn't try to put their two cents in every other minute."

"I bet; Dad is really bad about that." Deme giggles.

"So are Andrew and Zagreus." I laugh.

"How are things going with Zagreus?" She asks me with a small smirk on the corner of her mouth.

"It's going." I tell her and she pouts. "What?"

"I am stuck here with Dad and a million-year-old woman, Rose. I. Need. Details." She says pointedly and I can't help but laugh.

"Things are really good between us. I mean, I never expected it because I was so mad at him when we first left, but now..." I sigh, "I just don't want to ruin things, you know?"

"Yeah," She smiles, "I get that, but you won't."

"How do you know?" I ask.

"Because of the way he looks at you." She states.

I laugh, "and how does he look at me?" I ask her.

"Like you're magic." She smiles.

"I don't know what you're talking about." I look past her, at the wall behind her.

"I don't know." She shifts the camera again, "It's a lot of things, like the way he says your name, or when you are together it feels like electricity is flowing between the two of you." I blush at her words and look down. "I just hope that someday, someone loves me like that."

I look back up at her, "You will. Don't worry." I smile.

Deme and I talk for a little longer before she has to go for dinner, and we say our goodbyes. I sit outside a little longer thinking about all of the things we talked about. I hope she knows that I love her, and I miss her. I can't help but remember all the moments I was mean to her for stealing my clothes or cutting my favorite dolls hair and I didn't talk to her for a week straight. All of those moments feel so long ago but like they were yesterday at the same time, and I suddenly can't remember that last time I told her that I was proud of her. I had to grow up and become her parent when ours wouldn't, and I hope she knows that I don't blame her for that, I wouldn't trade that time together for the world.

I slip back inside the hotel room where the boys are still sitting exactly where I left them, watching some silly movie on the old tv in the room.

"Do you guys wanna take a look around?" I ask them.

"If you wanted to go play fetch at the park, all you had to do was ask." Andrew jokes.

"Rude." I tell him. "You can stay here then, like the prisoner you are." He throws a pillow at me, and I duck it.

"I mean, we still have a few hours to kill, so why not? Let's get some fresh air while we still can." Zagreus grabs a room key and slides it in his pocket and holds the door open. I grab a grey hoodie from my bag and meet him by the door.

"Are you coming 'Drew?" I ask.

"Only if you promise to never call me that again." He groans. "I can't believe I let that guy call me that." He shudders, gets up and follows us out the door.

The air is cool against my skin as we walk across the parking lot, we load up in the jeep and make the short drive to The Sands, a beach on the southernmost tip of Port Royal. The beach isn't very packed, which I imagine is only because it is still winter, and only a few families have their towels and umbrellas set up in the sand. I put my hoodie on, get out of the jeep, and head down to the water, with Zagreus and Andrew right behind me. We stand on the shore and take in the view.

"Did you know there's a Marine Corps base over there?" Andrew asks.

"I saw the signs for it on the way here." I tell him.

"My dad was stationed here before he transferred to Camp Pendleton in California." He tells us, "It's where they train the new recruits." He adds before getting quiet. I forgot that he hasn't seen his parents in a long time, they don't even know he is alive.

"You must miss them." I hold his hand and squeeze it; Andrew looks down at me and smiles.

"Yeah. Maybe…" He starts, "Maybe when this is all over, I'll get to see them again."

"You will." I tell him, "Once the full moon is here and you become human again, you can go anywhere you want again. No more sunlight or diet restrictions." I tease him.

"We're going to have to come up with one hell of a story for his return though." Zagreus adds. "Maybe give him amnesia or something."

"Lost boy returns after surviving in the woods for ten months." I joke.

"No that's good, I like that. It's front-page material." Andrew laughs. "I can see it now; I'll be the talk of the town."

"All the girls at school will want to be *with* you, and all the boys will want to *be* you." I laugh.

"Except for me, I'm good." Zagreus smiles and squeezes my shoulder.

"Me too." Andrew sighs, "There's only one girl out there for me."

"Gabby will be so happy when we get back." I assure him.

"I'm gonna marry that girl." Andrew states, Zagreus and I turn to look at him. "Even if I don't become human again and we have to send the rest of our lives working graveyard shifts and hunting deer." He adds, and I squeeze his hand again.

"It won't come to that; we'll find a way to cure you, even if Selene doesn't." I tell him, "Wont we, Zagreus?"

"Yeah." He says, "We will."

"Hey look," Andrew bends down and picks something up off the ground, he holds it out in his hands to show us, "Shark tooth." He says proudly.

"We should turn that into an amulet for you." Zagreus says.

"An amulet?" Andrew asks.

"Yeah, like the one I gave Rose." He grabs my hand and holds it up, showing Andrew the black leather band with the moonstone and wolf pendants that hangs from my wrist.

"This is an amulet?" I ask him.

"Yeah, I made it for you when I realized that you weren't going to stop putting yourself in immediate danger. It helps keep you protected." He explains, I look at the moonstone shimmering as it hangs. "The moonstone is meant to provide inner peace, intuition, balance and protection."

"What is the wolf for?" I ask him.

"It's because you're a wolf." He answers, "I thought you'd like it more with that on there." He explains.

"Well thanks." I smile.

"Shark teeth are a symbol of strength and protection, I could make you a bracelet too, or a necklace if you'd prefer." Zagreus offers Andrew.

"That would be cool dude, thanks." Andrew hands him the shark tooth.

"What makes it an amulet?" I ask Zagreus.

"It's been blessed by a god." He smirks.

At sundown, we walk into the Mermaids Grotto. It is a small building, with décor that looks like it comes from the area, seashell chandeliers and sun-bleached wooden tables. In a way it reminds me of the coffee shop I used to work at in Paradise. The layouts of both places are almost identical, each with a large counter in front of the kitchen, and tables strewn about the rest of the room. A stage is setup in the far side of the room, with a mounted tv, speakers, and microphones laid out on a barstool. We get seated at a table along the wall, nearest the exit, by a teenage girl with blue hair. She hands us menus, takes our drink order, and walks back to the kitchen to get started. Within the hour, the room begins to fill with all sorts of people and their conversations blend as they all speak at the same time.

Eventually the karaoke starts, and alcohol flows out to the tables as the people work up the courage to sign up. Some of them are good, but like usual with karaoke, most of the songs are mediocre. One act after the other goes up to the stage and performs. We hear love songs, pop songs, break up ballads, and too many power ballads. By the time nine o'clock rolls around I have a headache and we still haven't heard the siren.

"Did you hear that?" Andrew asks us.

"Hear what?" I rub my temple and Zagreus looks around.

"They have unlimited fries!" Andrew exclaims, "I'm gonna order more."

"This is pointless." I groan.

"I mean I could eat fries all night, but if you think so maybe I won't order more then."

"Not the fries." I roll my eyes, "*This.*" I wave my hands around. "The siren isn't here, and they are closing soon. We should just look for another lead." I tell the boys.

"I'm going to ask for the check." Zagreus tells us, getting up from the table and walking to the hosts stand. I rest my head on the table and close my eyes.

"Do you hear that?" Andrew asks me.

"I don't hear anything Andrew." I reply, but he doesn't say anything. After another minute of no response from him I open my eyes to find him gone. I sit up and look around. I don't see Andrew anywhere and I don't see Zagreus either. I get up from the table and walk up to the blue haired girl that sat us. "Hey, did you see where the boys I came in with went?" I ask her.

"Nope." She shakes her head and walks off to a table. I decide to check the bathrooms. A man walks out of the men's room as I walk up. "I'm sorry, you didn't happen to see a tall guy with locs walk in there did you?" He shakes his head and walks past me.

I head outside and listen for them, but I don't hear anything other than a few people standing by their cars smoking. I pick a random direction and walk, hoping to rid the smoke from my nose so I might be able to pick up on either of the boy's scent. My footsteps crunch in the gravel as I walk over to a secluded area covered by trees. I look around and I still don't see anything, but I catch the slight smell of Zagreus's cologne and follow the direction its coming from. I walk for a few minutes into the darkness, not sure where I'm going nor what I'm going to find when I get there. They wouldn't have just wondered off without saying anything to me, that's my thing. A branch breaks ahead of me, and I pick up the pace.

I walk into a clearing of trees, Andrew is right in front of me, walking steadily towards Zagreus, whose hand is being pulled by a small, stick of a girl with dark auburn hair. She catches sight of me and begins to run, Zagreus and Andrew match her pace and continue to follow her. I run after them, getting hit in the face with branches and moss as I run through the shrubbery. When I finally break through the bushes, I'm standing on a beach, and she is leading them towards the water. Her mouth is moving, like she is speaking to them or maybe singing, but I can't hear anything, just my own breathing and the sound of the waves crashing on the sand. I break into a run, she has nowhere to go but the water, and the waves are so angry they would just push her back towards the shore. I reach her just as she reaches the water, I punch her square in the face, and she falls to the ground. That seems to snap the boys out of her trance and they both stop moving.

"Where..." Zagreus looks around, "Where are we?"

"You were being led to your death by a siren until I punched her in the face." I glare at them both, "You're welcome." I turn back to the siren and grab her arm, pulling her to her feet.

"You want to tell me what the hell is going on here?" I ask her. she is admittedly pretty, with blue eyes and freckles that dot her nose. A red mark is forming on her cheek where I punched her.

"I...I..." She hesitates and reaches up to feel her cheek.

"Oh man," I man laughs from behind us, "I knew I was going to like this girl." I turn my head to get a look at the man. Poseidon stands behind us, smiling widely. "You guys really missed out, wolfy here just landed a solid on this sea witches face." He makes his way over to us and pats me on the shoulder.

"I have a name." I tell him, and Zagreus looks at me with his eyes wide.

"Course you do, sweetheart." He blows me off and faces the girl, "Now you, tell me where my trident is, or I'll sick the bloodsucker on you next."

"T... tt...trident?" She stutters still clutching her face with the hand I'm not currently squeezing to keep her from running away.

"*Ta...ta...ta...*" Poseidon mocks her, "Yes, the trident you stole from me. *Tell me where it is.*" He growls at her. The ocean seems to respond to his anger, waves begin crashing one after the other, spraying us with a mist. Being this close to Poseidon makes me feel small, but I try not to focus on his arm muscles as he rolls up his sleeves. The girl is shaking in my grasp, obviously terrified.

"I didn't... I didn't mean to..." She starts.

"Didn't mean to what?" He barks, getting right up in her face.

"I didn't mean to offend you sir, I only wanted..." She looks down, "I was hoping to use it and return it." This causes him to burst out laughing.

"Use it? You thought you would use it." He laughs, "You? A mere pest, thought you could wield the power of a god and what?" he puckers his lips like he is thinking, "Let's take a guess, Wolf-girl, what do you suppose this barnacle brain wanted to use the trident for." I ignore his wolf comment and look at the girl, she looks at me for a moment before turning her attention back to the towering god in front of her.

"To make herself human." I answer him.

"Ding, ding, ding, we have a winner!" He claps his hands slowly in the girls' face, with each clap it feels like the ground is shaking. "You'll be lucky if I turn you into a polyp after this." He spits. Tears slide down her face, they shimmer in the moonlight like they are made from glitter. "Now, I'm going to ask you *one more time.*" He stands up straight in front of her. "Where is the trident?" he asks. She is still shivering, still crying, but she closes her eyes, and when she opens them again, the tears stop.

"The sea stack in the water." She speaks. I look past her towards the ocean and spot a rock-formation far out into the water. Poseidon spots it too and grins, He pushes her to the side, and she falls to the ground next to me. As he approaches the water's edge, the ocean parts for Poseidon, and he walks right through it. Zagreus moves to me, and so does Andrew but I'm frozen in place. I have never seen anything like it, as Poseidon trudges through the bottom of the ocean, moving elegantly until he reaches the rocks. The ocean obeys him, and he begins to climb the water like a staircase, until he reaches the top and puts his hand inside. Poseidon pulls the trident from the rock sea stack and holds it up in the air in victory. The ocean crashes around him, completely covering him, and when I blink my eyes, he is standing back in front of me.

Poseidon stands taller than before, the trident gripped tightly in his right hand. The trident is massive, the three-pronged fishing spear rests at least two feet taller than I am, and it is made of gold that shines in the light of the moon. He looks down at the girl with the heat of one thousand suns, like he is thinking about all the ways he can punish her.

"Leave us." Poseidon shouts. None of us move but Zagreus grabs my wrist. "You have aided me in the return of my trident, and I will fulfill my end of our deal. Call upon me when you must and not a moment earlier." He commands.

"How do—" I begin, Poseidon cuts me off by tossing something to me. I catch it and look at my hands. It is a cone shaped shell the size of a whistle, white in color with brown dots that are almost square in shape and an unusually high spire.

"Blow into this and I will come." He assures me, "Now leave the girl and do not look back." He warns us, his voice low but not quite a growl. Zagreus pulls me by my wrist and grabs Andrew's as well, leading us back towards the direction of the jeep. I look back briefly when we reach the tree line, Poseidon stands over the siren, his trident pointed directly at her, I look away from the scene.

I couldn't hear the sirens song, but I could hear her screams.

6

In The Shadows

The car barrels down the open road. Sixty, seventy, eighty miles an hour. The trees blur into one another, the dotted lines in the middle of the road morph into one. Rain hits the windshield like shrapnel, the wipers swing violently back and forth at the droplets. Zagreus doesn't let up on the gas for even a second until we are miles and miles away from Port Royal. None of us speak a word. All I can hear is the sound of the siren's scream echoing in my skull.

"Pull over." I say quietly. For a moment I'm not sure if he heard me but the car slows, and bounces as we pull over to the side of the road. Zagreus hits the lights and turns off the jeep, surrounding us in shadows and moonlight. I throw the door open and practically fall to the ground. I cough and cry until I throw up. Footsteps crunch in the dirt, rounding the car and walking up to my side.

"Rose, are you alright?" Zagreus kneels next to me, placing a hand delicately on my back as I dry heave.

"Do..." I breathe heavily, "Do I look alright to you?" He pulls my hair back, pulling it away from my face as I fall forward on the palms of my hands and throw up again.

"Andrew, can you hand me a bottle of water from the cooler behind my seat?" Zagreus calls back, a moment later I can hear the plastic bottle transfer between them before Zagreus takes the cap off and holds it out to me. "Here, drink this." I shake my head as I dry heave more. My throat burns too much from the stomach acid to speak. "Please?" He begs, "It'll help." He tells me. I relent and take a sip. I can feel the water go down all the way to my stomach.

"Why did he do that?" I whisper to the ground in front of me. Zagreus either doesn't hear me or doesn't know how to answer. "Why did he do that?" I ask louder.

"She..." He trails off, I search for the answer in his eyes. "She stole from a god." He speaks. "And not just any god, she stole from one of the big three." He tries to justify, but I can tell he doesn't agree with what he is saying.

"Is this what it was like before?" I breathe.

"What do you mean?"

"Is this what it was like when the gods could interfere with mortal lives?"

"At times." He answers honestly. I look up at him and can see the regret in his eyes.

"It can't be like this." I tell him.

"It won't be." He assures me, "We will be better this time."

"How can you promise something like that?" I narrow my eyes.

"He can't." A woman's voice answers me. I turn towards the voice and find a tall figure, shrouded in a long black cloak that covers her face. In one hand she holds a burning torch, in the other is a chain attached to a very skinny black dog.

"Who are you?" I ask, taking Zagreus's hand and slowly standing. She reaches up with both hands and slowly lowers the cloak from her head. Her long dark hair hangs loosely, her fair skin reflects the orange light of the torch, and her eyes are as dark as the night.

"I am Hecate." She speaks, her voice calm and clear.

"Why are you here?" I ask her.

She smiles sweetly, "You are at a crossroads." I look around and she giggles, "Not literally. Metaphorically."

"What do you mean?" Zagreus asks her.

"The girl has a decision to make." She explains. "Tell me your name." She says to me.

"My name is Rose."

"Walk with me Rose." She extends her hand that is holding the chain out to me, I hesitate.

"Why can't you talk here?" Zagreus asks her.

"Animals are meant to roam free, are they not? I believe the wolf wishes for the comforts only the wilderness can provide." She explains to him, "You are both welcome to join us if you wish." I hadn't noticed Andrew get out of the car; he stands behind us.

Zagreus locks the car and Hecate leads us down a path into the forest. We walk silently among the trees, crickets and cicadas singing to the night sky around us, until we reach a small fire where Hecate motions for us to sit. The dog lays at her feet as she places the torch into the flames of the fire and sits on a fallen tree. The boys and I sit on another log across from her. The warmth of the fire spreads over my body, I hadn't even realized I was shivering.

"You do not wish to be on this path," She says, "After the horrors you witnessed, I do not blame you. The path you walk is treacherous, and I am afraid your latest encounter will not be the worst you will see." Her face changes, morphing into another and quickly back.

"You can see the future." Zagreus says.

"I see all, past, present, and yes, future. The world shows me each direction. The fate of all who have come, those who are, and those who will." She nods, "This is of course, why I am here with you now."

"I don't understand." I tell her.

"A decision lies before you." She turns to me, "Two paths, one leading deeper down the path you currently follow, the other a way out."

"But why me?" I ask her desperately.

"If not you, another would have emerged eventually. The universe always finds a way."

"So, what you're saying is that..." I trail off.

"Had you not challenged Ares, another would have." She confirms what I was thinking.

"So, it isn't my fault." I sigh.

Zagreus looks at me, "Is that really what you thought?" He asks me.

"I... I mean..." I close my eyes and take a deep breath. "Yes, I did." Zagreus takes my hand in his and runs his thumb over the back of mine. Hecate observes us quietly.

"But wait, are you saying what I think you are? That there is a way out of this?" I ask her.

"Yes." She answers.

"How?" Andrew asks this time.

"You return home. You do not continue this quest." For some reason, her answer doesn't feel right to me.

"But we've already come so far." I tell her, "What happens if we just go home now?"

"I cannot answer that."

"What if we continue? Can you tell us that?" I ask, holding my breath.

"I cannot." She states, "I can only tell you what comes next based on your decision." I look up at the sky, frustrated. I am sick and tired of everyone running me around like a chicken with its head cut off. Why can't they just be up front and tell me? Why does it have to be *my* decision? I close my eyes and focus on the sound of the fire as it crackles. I listen to the crickets singing, and the dog breathing heavily next to Hecate.

"I don't know what to do." I say to no one.

"Many moons ago, a friend had to make a very similar decision." Hecate says, I open my eyes and look at her. "She was faced with two choices, live her life as told by her mother, or follow her heart to the man of her dreams." She explains.

"My mother." Zagreus whispers.

"Yes, Zagreus." She smiles sweetly at him. "Persephone was torn between her old life and the one she longed for. She could have denied your father, lived a simple life with her mother, still happy. But she chose the unknown. She followed her heart." Her words echo around us in the darkness.

We really have come a long way, and if I were to go home now, what would it all have been for? Andrew might not have ever become a vampire sure, but I would still be a wolf. Deme would still be an oracle. Phoenix would never have come home, and neither would the other wolves. Would my dad be alive, or would he have drunk himself to death by now? Who knows what could have happened, maybe I wouldn't have fallen in love, wouldn't have become friends with Gabby or Aphrodite.

"We can't go back." I say quietly.

Hecate rises to her feet, the black dog rising with her. Her face begins to darken and change, her eyes changing from green to dark black before rolling into the back of her head. The fire grows stronger as she begins to speak in an entirely different voice. *"A dark son will rise, consumed in hate. As a father takes fall, a sacrifice made. Untamed Fury, bound in chains, a tomb of bronze, will seal his fate."* The fire goes out completely, leaving us in complete darkness. To my right, I can feel Zagreus moving, he pulls his phone from his pocket and turns on the flashlight. He uses the light to look around, the fire is gone, with no evidence of embers, or even smoke. When he points the flashlight to where Hecate was a moment ago, she is gone.

"Someone has to say it, so it might as well be me." Andrew says quietly, "She's got *style*." He nods his head approvingly. I jump when a raven lands on the fallen tree in front of us, the bird looks at all three of us individually, turning its head before croaking three times and flying off into the night sky.

"We should get out of here." Zagreus tells us, an urgency behind his tone and we run back to the jeep as fast as we can through the brush.

When we get back to the jeep my phone won't stop going off, I have ten missed calls, each accompanied by a voicemail, and sixteen—seventeen texts telling me to answer my phone, all of them from my dad. I dial the number back and put the call on speaker phone, placing it on the center console. Zagreus, Andrew, and I huddle together over my phone.

"Rose. Are you there?" My dad answers.

"Yeah, dad. You're on speakerphone with Zagreus, Andrew, and me. You'll never guess what just happened." I tell him.

"Listen to me, your sister just had another vision."

"She did?" I look up at Zagreus and he nods. "Did she say anything?" I ask.

"It was some kind of riddle, or prophesy maybe."

"A dark son will rise." I repeat Hecate's words.

"How did you know?" He asks.

"Never mind that. What do you think it means?"

"I was hoping Zagreus would know." My dad answers.

"It can mean a lot of things. The words of a prophet can be interpreted a million different ways." Zagreus explains, shaking his head. "I don't have any idea what the first two lines can be, I mean, do we know if they mean sun or son?" He scratches his head as he thinks it through, "The darkest day of the year is during winter solstice though and it would have been a couple weeks ago, so if we go by that logic maybe they mean son, like a child. But even then, whose son? It could mean any one of us, Nix, Andrew, Ares, even me."

"We should assume it's Ares." I say, "I mean that's who we are trying to stop after all."

"And if we assume its Ares, then the next line would make the father, Zeus." Andrew adds.

"The next part is where it gets tricky. *A sacrifice made* could mean anything." Zagreus tells us.

"Didn't you tell us that sacrifices used to be made to the gods? Could it be that?" I ask.

"Without more context, it is difficult to know. It could mean animal sacrifice, but it could also be a sacrifice of power, of life, anything really."

"Let's skip that part then." My dad tells us, "Go on to the next."

"Untamed fury could be another reference to Ares, meaning he ends up in chains." Zagreus states.

"*a tomb of bronze will seal his fate.*" I repeat. "Does that mean we need to find a tomb built with bronze and inside it could be the weapon we need to take him down?"

"The second part could be true, but tombs aren't generally built from bronze." My dad answers.

"What about a tomb with a bronze door?" Andrew asks.

"I mean, there might be one out there, but I don't think that's what it means." Zagreus tells us. "But I don't know what else it could be."

"But where does all of this leave us?" I groan, sinking down in my seat. "And what about that creepy raven?"

"Creepy raven?" My dad asks, I can almost see the skeptical face he is making through the sound of his voice.

"The raven wasn't a part of it." Zagreus answers.

"Then what? It was just a random chance encounter?" Andrew raises his brow.

"No. Ravens are how Hermes gathers his intel and delivers his messages to the gods." Zagreus explains.

"So, you speak raven?" Andrew asks.

Zagreus rolls his eyes but doesn't answer his question. Instead, he says, "The raven was delivering a warning. We should assume that everything we know, Ares does too; he may even know more."

"So, you *do* speak raven." Andrew mutters under his breath.

"Dad?" I sit up and lean back over the phone.

"Yes?"

"How is Deme?" I ask, "Is she okay after this last vision?"

"Deme has recovered surprisingly fast. She is resting now, but..." He trails off.

"But what?" I ask.

"We are coming home." He tells me. "Deme needs the comfort of her own bed."

"But what about the oracle, if she is helping her, why would you leave?"

"The oracle will be joining us." He sighs, "I'll explain everything more soon. I don't feel comfortable giving Deme her phone back yet but seeing you might make her feel better. If you can, you should come home too." The way my father says this makes me more homesick than I want to admit. I look up at Zagreus but the look he gives me, tells me that he doesn't know when we will be able to return.

"I'll try." I tell him.

We say our goodbyes and hang up, Zagreus starts the jeep and pulls back onto the road. "Where are we going?" I ask him, snapping my seatbelt into place across my body.

"Well, I don't know about you guys, but there is only one person I know who might know something about a bronze tomb." Zagreus tells us. "Hephaestus."

"Doesn't he like, hate Ares?" Andrew asks.

"That's putting it *lightly*." Zagreus laughs, "So, even if he doesn't know anything about it, we might find ourselves another ally anyway. Plus, it just so happens, I'm pretty sure heading towards him will put us back on track for home. But I might have to make a quick phone call to make sure he's where I think he is."

"No. No way. *Absolutely not*. I will not tell you where Hephaestus is!" Aphrodite shrieks through the phone. We are parked at a gas station somewhere off the highway. Zagreus is inside getting snacks, and while Andrew hides in the backseat from the sun, I sit on the hood of the jeep soaking in the sunlight while I can, trying to coax Hephaestus's location from Aphrodite.

"Oh, come on." I roll my eyes at her. "You owe me."

"*Owe you?*" She scoffs, "Please, a goddess does not owe anyone anything."

"Let's see," I hold the phone to my ear with my shoulder and begin counting on my fingers, "Your ex-boyfriend sicked a chimera on me and I almost died, you moved in with my family for free when you can apparently afford a *penthouse* in New Orleans, you hid the existence of the Vry from us, and you get to sit on your pretty butt all day while I travel around the country with two smelly boys. I think you owe me." Aphrodite is quiet for a moment.

"You know, I didn't ask for any of this." She whines.

"Maybe not," I tell her, watching Zagreus as he makes his way over to me. "But you are going to tell me anyway."

"Fine." She finally relents. I shoot a thumbs up at Zagreus as he approaches me. "You didn't hear this from me though, okay?"

I roll my eyes again, and put the phone on speaker, "If he asks, you have my word I won't tell him it was you who told us."

"Thank you." She says smugly, "He is in some volcano, in Colorado. I think it's near an important river or something." She goes on, rambling about some lake with a waterfall that has fish that eat the dead skin off from peoples' feet. "Or is that in the middle east?" She asks.

"You're getting a little off topic here, Aph." I blink, Zagreus rolls his eyes and leans back against the jeep next to me, he hands me a stick of beef jerky.

"You're right" She laughs, "But like I said, it's a volcano in Colorado." Zagreus pulls out his phone and types volcano into the search-bar. After he searches for a moment, he shows me the screen.

"Is it called Dotsero?" I ask her.

"Probably."

"Aph, please.

"Okay, okay, yes. I believe it is called Dotsero. Happy?" She grumbles.

"Yes, thank you!" I tell her, hanging up the phone before she can talk my ear off about something else.

Zagreus turns and faces me; I scoot to the edge of the hood and frown at him.

"Thanks for doing that." He tells me. "There was no way she was going to tell me."

"I know, I just wish she wasn't so..." I trail off looking for the right word.

"Annoying, bitchy, stuck-up, airheaded?" He offers, "take your pick, I could go all day."

"Come on, you know what I mean. Everything just has to be so difficult with her."

"Did you expect any less?" He asks, putting a hand on my knee.

"I mean, no." I take his hand in mine. "What's the story with you two anyway?"

"Me and Aphrodite? There is no story." He answers, "At least, not officially, anyway." He smiles. I roll my eyes and drop his hand; He looks at me like he's offended.

"Tell me the story, then." I cross my arms.

"Like I said, there isn't a story." He tells me, but I raise my eyebrows and look the other way. "Okay fine. Aphrodite tends to want to be in the middle of everything. I mean, literal wars were started because of her." He rolls his eyes and leans into me; I wrap my legs around him and listen intently. "Of course, she would end up being the goddess of love, it just makes sense. Always trying to set people up, always trying to figure out who peoples soulmates are."

"Did she try to set you up with someone."

"Multiple someone's." He answers honestly, "But I never took the bait. I mean for the sake of honesty, I did once or twice. And don't look at me like that because we are talking years—eons before now."

"Didn't you say you were younger than me once?" I tease him.

"I am. Well, technically my body is—do you want to hear the story or not?" He asks and I pretend to zip my lips shut. "Thank you. Anyway, Aphrodite eventually tried to get my attention herself."

I unzip my lips, "*Aphrodite* tried to seduce *you*?" I ask wide eyed, he cringes.

"Seduce is such a harsh word, but yes." He agonizes.

"Oh. My. God."

"Tell me about it," He groans, "But nothing ever felt right. I guess that's when she realized she didn't have any power over me and declared me 'unlovable' and she has hated me ever since." He shrugs.

I take his face in my hands, "First of all, you are not *unlovable*, and second, oh my god!" I squeeze his cheeks together and then lay flat on my back. "It all makes so much sense now."

"What does?" He asks.

"Why Ares hates you too, for starters." I sit back up, "and why she told me that I don't have a soulmate."

"Wait, she told you that."

"Well not exactly. But you know..." I trail off.

"No, I don't know. Tell me."

"Okay, she did tell me that I don't have one, then she said she couldn't tell who yours was but had her assumptions." I explain.

"Huh." Zagreus says like he just realized something.

"What?"

"Well, if she has no power over me. It makes sense that she wouldn't have any power over my soulmate either." He tells me.

"So does that mean you think we're soulmates?" I ask.

"Oh, I know we are." He leans in and kisses me sweetly.

"Get a room!" Andrew calls from the backseat, causing me to blush. Zagreus helps me down off the hood of the jeep and we get in. "Do we know where we're going yet?" Andrew asks as Zagreus starts the car up.

"Colorado." I answer him pulling up a map on my phone and inputting the directions.

Andrew groans, "Can we just get plane tickets or something?"

"Let me get this straight." Zagreus looks at him in the rearview mirror, "You crave literal human blood, Rose is a straight up wolf, and you want to get on a plane, where anything could happen, including but not limiting to, Ares shooting it down?"

"He hasn't come after us yet."

"That doesn't mean he won't. And I'm not leaving my jeep here, the moisture could cause rust." Zagreus tells him, for the most part I'm ignoring them though as I look at the map on my phone.

"Hey guys?" I ask them, they both give me their attention, "Do you think we could make a pitstop?"

"Aren't we already at a gas station? Use the bathroom here." Andrew tells me.

"Not for that," I hold up my phone screen for them to see, "For this?"

Zagreus takes the phone and observes the map, "Yeah I think we can manage that." He answers.

7

Big Bad Wolf

The drive from South Carolina to Colorado is almost exactly twenty-four hours, but we aren't going to Colorado, at least not yet anyway. Instead about halfway through the trip we change course and move north towards Black River Falls, Wisconsin. I didn't tell Phoenix we were coming. I figured that if I had, he would try to tell me not to, that he was fine without his little sister. But having not heard from him in a while, I needed to make sure he was okay, and he needed to know that Deme was going home.

The forest is dense on either side of the highway. As we drive through it, I can't help but be reminded of Paradise, of the forests I call home, and I wonder if that is why Nix hasn't contacted anyone. It never occurred to me that he might like it here, maybe even more than home. Zagreus pulls into a parking lot on the side of the highway, a gateway sign reads that this is where the campground to Black River Falls Forest is. Campers and RVs are parked throughout the area, I can hear an ATV engine running loudly somewhere in the forest. My heart beats furiously, begging my body to step foot in the clean air, to run through the trees and wildlife. It almost feels involuntary how much my body wants to turn into a wolf right now.

"Rose, are you okay?" Andrew asks, "I can hear you panting from back here."

"What?" I try to compose myself, "Yeah, I'm okay."

"Why don't you stick your head out the window to cool off." Andrew jokes, I turn and give him a dirty look.

"Do you have a problem?" I ask him.

"Nope, no problem here." He puts his hands up in surrender. "You can stick your tongue out while you do it too, I hear dogs like that."

"When is the next full moon? Cause maybe when he is human again, he'll stop with all these offensive dog jokes" I ask Zagreus.

"Another week, and you guys seriously need to cool it. This is going to be a very long week if you guys don't start getting along again."

"I'm not the one being a bitch." Andrew states and Zagreus slams on the breaks sending him flying into the back of my seat.

"What did you just say?" Zagreus turns to him.

"It was just a joke..." Andrew rubs his head and Zagreus cuts him off.

"That wasn't a joke, it was an insult." He looks like he might punch Andrew, "Take it back and tell Rose that you're sorry."

"I'm... I'm sorry Rose, I didn't mean it like that..." Andrew starts.

"It's fine. Don't worry about it." I tell him. Zagreus doesn't look satisfied, but he turns around anyway and continues driving through the parking lot, his knuckles are white from clutching the steering wheel so hard.

Walking through the forest reminds me of when Zagreus took me to the cliffs after that night at the party. He walks in front, Andrew trailing behind him. I follow behind them both, taking in as much of the fresh air and the scenery as I can. The boys haven't spoken to each other since we parked the car and I could cut the tension between them with a knife, but I don't say anything either. Instead, I focus on the wind as it blows across my face, the short grass as it tickles at my ankles, the textures of the leaves as I run them through my fingers. I could stay out here forever.

As Zagreus and Andrew continue ahead of me, I take a moment to myself and close my eyes. Focusing on my brother, I remember the way his room smells, his spray bottle cologne that tickles my nose, the way his voice sounds and the way he drags his feet across the carpet in the hallway every morning. The connection between us thins and I can feel him, as though he is standing right next to me. He is breathing normally, smelling the same cool air that I am. There are others near him, I can hear a can as it is crushed and thrown into a pile of others, I can hear laughter and then I can hear my brother.

"Get out of my head, Rose." He growls and instantly the connection is severed. I open my eyes and the boys are both standing in front of me.

"Sorry, I was just—" I start, but Zagreus interrupts me.

"Did you find him." He asks.

"Yeah, I think so." I nod, "Follow me."

I lead the boys down a trail that takes us deeper into the forest. We begin to see wildlife of all sorts. Elk cross a river a few yards away, squirrels climb trees, shaking their tails at us and birds dig in the dirt, scavenging for food. But there is something else, something I don't recognize. It feels like we are being followed, I can feel eyes on me with every step I take, like I am being hunted. But I don't hear whatever it is following us, it's footsteps never approach, and it stays far enough away that I can't catch the scent either.

I am so distracted trying to find this thing, that I don't even realize I walked right into a trap until the metal teeth are already clutching my ankle. I scream and fall to the ground. Zagreus runs up to me, but before he can pull the steel jaws out of my skin he freezes in place, holding his hands up in the air.

"Who are you?" A voice asks, through my tears I try to make out the figure in front of us, but the most I can tell is that he is tall and built like a truck, and he is holding something to Zagreus's head. Zagreus doesn't speak, nor does Andrew, but the pain in my leg is so unbearable I can't help but continue to cry out. I can feel blood on my hands as I clutch my leg, this makes me panic more.

"Rose?" A familiar voice speaks, "What the fuck, Steele, that's my sister!" Phoenix yells, I hear footsteps approach rapidly, but the figure in front of me and Zagreus doesn't even flinch. "Oh my god, seriously!" Nix exclaims. "Put that stupid thing down and help me get this off her!" He pushes the arm of the figure away and bends down next to me. "Rose, I need you to be very still, okay? I know this is going to hurt, but big deep breaths and try not to move." He tells me, before whispering something to Zagreus that I can't hear through my cries. Someone ties something to the top of my calf and squeezes it tightly.

Is that a tourniquet?

Oh god. I'm going to lose my leg.

Someone messes with the chain attached to the bear trap, making me feel woozy with the movement.

"Stay with us Rose, okay? I need you to be very still. Zagreus will pull your leg out when he can, just don't make any quick movements." Nix talks to me, but he sounds like he is miles away from me and I can barely hear what he is saying. I focus hard, trying to listen to him and keep still but my leg burns. He counts down from three and I feel the jaws loosen, then open completely, a pair of hands pull me out of the trap and drags me away from it before I hear the metal snap back together.

There is movement all around me, three maybe four bodies surround mine, but I can't see what they are doing. My vision begins to black out from the pain. I focus hard, squinting my eyes and rubbing them. I can hear someone breathing heavily, "That's a lot of blood." Andrew speaks and the last thing I see is Zagreus pick up Andrew and throw him before I black out entirely.

I am in a tent when I wake up. Groggily I look around, before I remember what happened to my leg and reach for it. I wince as I feel my ankle. Yes, it's still there, and my foot, I wiggle my toes, everything is still there. I lay back down and take in the pain. It still hurts, and it feels like it is throbbing under the bandages that are wrapped around it. I sit up and look at my hands, they are covered in dry blood, along with my shorts and the bare skin of my legs. I wince as I get up, careful not to put any weight on my leg, as I exit the tent. I use a tree next to the tent to pull myself up with until Zagreus catches sight of me and rushes to my side.

"Careful." He whispers, wrapping my arm around his neck and lifting me into his arms. "You should have called for help."

"I know." My voice is hoarse, probably from the screaming. "Where are we?" I ask him. There are mostly tents, but a small RV is also parked close by, with a small fire burning next to it and a group of people gathered around sitting in fold out chairs. Zagreus carries me to the group of people and slowly places me in one of the chairs before pulling his own chair in front of mine and putting my legs in his lap. Phoenix is sitting next to me, a small girl with curly brown hair and a button nose sits on the other side of him, the built guy is sitting on the steps in front of the RV door and next to Zagreus is a tan-skinned kid no older than twelve; I don't see Andrew anywhere. "Where are we?" I repeat.

"You're at our camp." Nix answers, handing me a bottle of water, "This is Lily, Steele and Peter." He points to each of them, Lily smiles sweetly and stretches over Nix to offer me her hand, I shake it and nod. Peter, the boy sitting next to Zagreus shyly looks up at me and waves, while Steele doesn't even ac-knowledge me, instead he whittles a tree branch to a point with a small knife.

"Where is Andrew?" I ask, Zagreus looks wary, but Nix looks angry.

"He's in there, with Alistair." Nix points at the RV, I didn't notice the lights were on.

"Rose, you should know." Zagreus starts, "Andrew would never mean to hurt you."

"What?" I ask confused.

"His instincts just took control." He continues, "When he saw all that blood, he just lost control."

"What are you saying to me?" I look at Nix for answers, but he looks away. My heart feels like it skips a beat.

"Andrew had some of your blood." Zagreus speaks slowly, but I shake my head.

"But that's okay, right?" I shake my head again, "Because I'm not human. I'm a wolf."

"*Part* wolf." Zagreus clarifies, "You are half human."

"No." I say quietly. "You don't mean..." I trail off.

"Andrew will, most likely, never be human again."

"No." I say again, tears building in my eyes. "No. He can't... He wouldn't..."

"He did." Nix says, his eyes locked straight ahead avoiding mine. I turn to Zagreus, searching for any sign that he is lying, I can't find one. Tears stream down my face.

This is my fault. If I hadn't suggested coming here, none of this would have happened. If I hadn't been so focused on trying to find out who was following us, I might have seen the bear trap and avoided it. He drank my blood. Andrew drank my blood and now he is a vampire for the rest of his life.

This is all my fault.

"Rose, listen. There is still a chance, maybe Selene will understand." Zagreus tries to comfort me. I bury my face in my hands. "He could still become human. We could look for some other way." He tries again but I don't want to listen to him.

I don't believe him. I want to run; I want out of this place. I should have gone home when we had the chance. Now I'm stuck here, with my leg torn up and my best friend a vampire.

"I want to go home." I blubber.

"Rose, we can't." Zagreus says delicately.

I look at him through my fingers, "Why not?"

"You need to heal, and Andrew can't be near humans right now."

"I feel fine." I tell him, I try to prove so by moving my leg, but I wince as I bump the heel of my foot against the armrest on his chair. The door of the RV clicks open, and Steele stands to get out of the way for a man who looks no older than my father. His black hair is pulled back into a ponytail that ends at the middle of his back and his features are sharp, but his eyes look kind. He closes the door behind him and joins us in front of the fire.

"The boy sleeps for now." Alistair speaks, his voice is deeper than I expected, "He was very distraught, so I gave him some chamomile tea." He announces before locking eyes with me. "You must be Rose." He extends his hand out to me; I shake it and nod. "It is very nice to meet you, though I do wish the circumstances were a little less *chaotic*." He gives Steele a very stern look.

"Any news? Can you tell if he's..." Nix asks before trailing off.

"The boy doesn't seem any different." Alistair answers, "You say he did not physically drink from the girl, correct?" Nix nods in response and Alistair continues, "I do not believe Andrew will transition any further than he already has. But of course, vampires are not my area of expertise."

"He didn't drink from me?" I ask, blinking the tears out of my eyes.

"No," Zagreus answers. I could hit him. "When we opened the bear trap, some of your blood splattered as it shut again and landed on Andrew. He had some of the blood that landed on him."

"It was pretty disgusting to watch actually." Nix adds, but him I can hit. I reach over and slap his arm, "Hey! What was that for?" He hollers.

"You jerks made it sound like he actually drank my blood!" I go to smack him again, but he moves his arm out of the way, and I hit the chair. "A drop doesn't matter, does it?" I turn to Zagreus.

"We don't know." Zagreus shakes his head, "Only time will tell."

"Then why did you tell me he would never be human again?"

"In case he doesn't. You need to be prepared to face it; Andrew might not be human ever again. And the thought of that nearly broke you. We needed to prepare you for when the time comes." Zagreus explains.

"You guys' suck at this." I sigh and wipe the tears from my face with my sleeve. I look down at myself and try to wipe at the dried blood on my legs.

"We should go get you a change of clothes." Zagreus says.

"Steele and I will walk with you back to your car," Nix tells him standing up and snapping his fingers at Steele who reluctantly gets up and follows him. Zagreus gets up slowly and places my foot back down on his chair delicately before reaching down and kissing the top of my head. The three of them disappear into the tree line.

Lily gets up, disappears into her tent for a moment and comes back carrying a small bag. She turns the chair Nix was sitting in to face me and sits down.

"Here, let me help you clean up." She smiles and pulls a package of wet wipes out of the bag. She pulls a wipe out and holds it up, "May I?" She asks and I nod. She begins wiping my face with it. "You and your brother look a lot alike." She tells me, throwing the wipe to the side and pulling out a new one before starting on the blood dried to my leg.

"We do?" I ask her, I've never thought about it too much.

"Yeah, you have the same mannerisms too." She giggles.

"You like him?" I ask and she blushes.

"Very much." She smiles, "He is very kind." I raise my brow and she laughs. "Once you get past his outer shell he is." She clarifies.

"Does he feel the same about you?" I ask her.

"I would hope so." She doesn't hesitate with her answer. Alistair and Peter begin pulling out pots and pans, setting them on a table where a propane grill sits. Lily continues to scrub the dried blood from my skin as the sun sinks lower and lower in the sky, covering us in a shadowy, orange glow.

When Zagreus returns, he is smiling and joking with my brother as they reemerge from the trees. It is dark out now, and lanterns light up the area around camp. Alistair shoves a bowl into my hand and smiles. It smells delicious; spicy, yet sweet.

"Just in time for some chili!" Alistair calls out to the boys. Steele comes over, grabs a bowl, and walks to a red tent before disappearing inside of it. Nix and Zagreus come over to the fire, dropping off our duffel bags next to me before grabbing a bowl each. I lift my foot off the chair and Zagreus sits down, I try to rest it on the ground by he insists I put it back on his lap.

"How was the walk?" Lily asks Nix, he smiles at her.

"Nice, learned a lot about what these guys have been up to in the last few days." Nix looks at me, "Must feel like it's been years since you've seen home."

"In ways." I answer after swallowing a spoonful of chili, it tastes better than it smells.

"You must have had so much fun though. I've lived here my whole life, so has Peter." Lily says, "I'd love to go on a road trip across the country." She sighs.

"I'll take you guys on one someday, babe." Nix tells her, I almost choke on my chili, and he laughs at me. "Lily and I are together." He smiles, reaching out and shakes her knee; I hope I don't look as red as she does when I blush. I give her an approving nod and she smiles at me.

"What is the craziest thing you've seen so far?" She asks. My face falls and I can hear the siren again, screaming loudly in my memories.

"We met Medusa." Zagreus tells her, distracting me from my own mind.

"That must have been so scary!" She exclaims.

"Actually, she was really nice." I tell her. "She even gave bought us some new clothes."

"Wow, I never would have guessed. Did she really have snakes for hair?"

"I don't know, she was wearing a scarf over her head." I shrug. "Can I actually ask you guys something?"

"Anything." Lily answers.

"What's the deal with Steele?" I look over at his tent, his lantern is dark.

"Steele is the newest addition to our camp." Alistair answers me. "He has had a troubled life, which has led to some unfortunate circumstances for him."

"What do you mean?" I ask.

"Steele was an orphan, and when he aged out of the system, he grew angry and distant from the world. Fell into the wrong crowd." Alistair explains vaguely, Lily and Nix exchange a look. "He means well, I assure you, but he is weary among strangers and has a lot of control to learn."

We all remain quiet for a moment before Lily breaks the silence, "Peter, why don't you head off to bed now?" The boy nods and sets his bowl down on the ground before making his way to a small yellow tent behind us. When he zips the tent shut Lily turns back to me, "Peter is my little brother. I was afraid to ask in front of him, but..." She trails off, thinking carefully about what she is going to say next, but Nix speaks before she can.

"Do you know how to stop Ares yet?" He asks.

"Maybe. We were on our way to find out when we decided to make the detour here first." Zagreus explains to them.

"I forgot to tell you, Nix. Dad and Deme are heading home." I tell him.

"Is she better?"

I nod, "Dad says she is."

"But you didn't talk to her?" he rolls his eyes.

"No, but shouldn't we go see her anyway?" I ask him. He doesn't say anything, but the look he is giving me says it all for him. "You aren't going back."

He shakes his head, "Can you blame me?" He asks. "I mean, there's nothing there for me anymore. Dad and I have never been close. And we both know I was never going to graduate high school." He adds, but he doesn't need to justify his decision to me.

"No." I say, I can tell he is going to say something else, but I put my hand up to stop him. "I don't blame you." I smile, "If you are happy here, then what else can I say?"

Nix smiles at me, and squeezes Lily's knee "Thank you."

"I'll let her know that you miss her." I tell him and he nods. "Hopefully we can head out soon though, I don't want to intrude more than we already have."

"You should be up and walking by tomorrow morning if you are as advanced as Phoenix tells me." Alistair tells me, "But you should get some rest and we will assess your wounds when you wake."

Crickets chirp, and somewhere outside of the tent I can hear an owl. After Zagreus carried me back to the tent and I changed out of my bloody clothes, I couldn't sleep. Everything replays in my brain like a tape on rewind. I find myself staring up at the moon through the top of the tent.

"Selene," I whisper, "If you can hear me. Please don't punish him, please. I beg you, let him become human again." Zagreus unzips the tent and crawls inside making me jump.

"You're still awake?" He asks, "You really should get some rest."

"I was waiting for you." I tell him and he kisses my forehead before laying down next to me. He gently wraps his arms around me and pulls me closer to him.

"How's your leg feeling?"

"Better." I tell him, he runs his fingers through my hair.

"You really scared me back there." He whispers, "I've never heard you scream like that before."

"That makes two of us," I laugh.

"But it made me more afraid of what's still to come."

"What do you mean?" I ask, turning around to face him.

"What if you get hurt again and I'm not there to help you." He says, his face falling. "If Ares lays a hand on you, I don't know what I'll do." He admits.

I kiss him softly, "Don't worry, I'll be okay." I tell him, closing my eyes and nuzzling up to his chest. He plays with my hair until I fall asleep.

The screams of the siren haunt my dreams until I wake up. I sit up in the complete darkness, the scream still ringing in my ears until I hear it again and realize that I'm not dreaming, and Lily is the one screaming. I lift myself up and climb over Zagreus, waking him in the process.

"Rose, go back to sleep." He says groggily, turning back over. I hastily unzip the door to the tent and am met with the warmth of a blazing fire. Zagreus sits up quickly behind me. I get to my feet, ignoring the pain in my ankle and try to make my way to Lily. The fire is burning the ground around the campsite, surrounding us entirely. Andrew bursts out from the RV with Alistair and instantly shields his eyes. Nix is now pulling Peter out from the yellow tent and Lily runs to them.

"What is going on?" Nix calls out to us. I look around, the fire is burning steadily, but it isn't traveling and there is one tent that isn't blocked in from the flames. I squint as I look at the tent Steele was sleeping in. I can barely make him out but then I see him, and he isn't alone.

"Ares." I whisper. Through the flames I can see him perfectly, the light dances around his face as his wicked grin spreads across his face. Steele stands next to him, but he doesn't look afraid; if anything, he looks as confident as Ares does. I take a step towards them, and then another until I reach a full sprint. My heart pounding in my chest I leap through the flames and land on the other side as a wolf.

"Rose!" Zagreus calls out, he runs after me, but the flames grow taller, blocking his way. Ares stands in front of me confident as ever. Half of his face illuminated as he begins to laugh. Next to him, Steele buckles, falling to the ground. His body is shifting, his bones crack and re-arrange themselves, the hair on his arms grows longer, his nails grow into claws. His body continues to mangle until standing in front of me is the biggest wolf I have seen. Steele's wolf form is even bigger than Phoenix's, he is easily twice the size of me and since men only transition into half-wolves, he has twice the range that I do. I'm not sure I can take him, maybe not even at full health, but that bear-trap didn't do me any favors.

Ares is just as big as I remember him, with bulging muscles and dark eyes. His dark hair waves in the wind as he stares daggers in my direction, in his hands is a spear. I inch towards him, taking in my options, but I don't have any. It is two against one. The spear tip glistens in the firelight, I know he is begging me to attack him so he can use it on me.

I growl deeply at him, and he laughs, "Oh no! I'm shaking in my boots." He chuckles, "What are you going to do? Huff, puff, *blow my house down*?" He mocks. "I should have finished you off after what you did to my chimera." Ares calls out. "I sure would have saved everyone from all this trouble. And look at how many people had to suffer because of you." He takes a step towards me, but I don't move. "I could just finish you off now," He mocks, "But that would be no fun, especially since you can't fight at full health. I mean, a bear trap. I just told the guy to embarrass you and he full on broke your leg! How impressive, I mean, the dedication to such brutality. That's my kind of bread and butter." He smirks, "That's right, Steele was on my side the entire time! Doesn't that just make you so angry?" Next to him, Steele doesn't move but I can feel the same energy radiating from him that comes from Ares too. I take another step forward. "Hold on little doggy, there will be plenty of time for fighting. And trust me, you won't want to miss what I have planned for you." The flames rise again, blinding me momentarily until they go out altogether, when my eyes adjust, Ares and Steele are gone.

Zagreus runs to me as I revert to my human form. When he reaches me, he envelopes me in his arms, holding me so tightly and not letting go.

"That was so reckless of you." He tells me, pulling away and holding my face in his hands. "I can't believe you did that." He kisses me quickly.

"Did you hear what he said?" I ask, pulling away from him.

"I did." He answers solemnly.

"Steele hurt me because Ares told him to. Who else could he have gotten to Zagreus?"

"I know, but darling we can't think like that." He tells me and I shake my head.

"Why not? He could follow us anywhere we go. He could hurt anyone at any moment, and we haven't done anything to stop him!" I yell. "We need to leave."

"We should wait until morning. He won't come back."

"No. We need to find Hephaestus and we need to *end this*." I tell him sternly, "We leave tonight, or I leave without you." I threaten.

8

Whose Side Are You On

The sun burns at my exposed skin as it hangs high in the clear sky. The rocky terrain of the mountainside makes it difficult to move quickly, especially with my injury from the bear trap, although the wound has healed drastically over the last day and a half, my ankle is still covered in bruises and puncture scars. Finding Hephaestus has been difficult, and it feels like we have hiked the canyon long enough to have done it twice. Zagreus doesn't speak to me. Occasionally he will reach out to help me across a wide gap or up a steep hill, but he hasn't said a single word since we left my brother. Neither has Andrew, who currently is sitting in the back of the Jeep, with air conditioning and a comfortable seat. I can't help but feel jealous of him as I bake in the heat.

Something is obviously wrong with the world. Colorado is supposed to be cold and snowy this time of year, but here I am, in shorts and a tank-top, sweating like I'm in the middle of the desert. The heat isn't the only difference I have noticed. The animals we pass seem to be uneasy, like they don't know where to go, elk and deer run away from nature and into the cities we pass. The people we encounter at gas stations are more irritable and angrier with each other, at one gas station someone pulled a gun on a mother and her daughter for walking in front of their car. A large man on the side of the road, carried a sign that said the world was ending, and the worst part was that he was right; it really did feel like the world was ending.

My mind spins as I remember everything I've been told over the last week. *If it hadn't been me, it would have been someone else,* I try to repeat to myself. But it doesn't feel true. It feels like the second I remembered who I was, was the moment that set all of this in motion.

My foot slips and I fall into a hole. Zagreus rushes to me and pulls me out, when my leg is free, I realize that this is the closest we have been in days, not including sitting next to one another in the car ride here. I want to say something to him, but the words never come and before I know it, Zagreus is already heading up the mountain.

As the sun sets, we still aren't any closer to finding out where on this mountain Hephaestus is currently hiding and I'm starting to think that the intel Aphrodite told us is incorrect. I take a second and look around, a flash of light catches my attention.

"Zagreus!" I call out, he turns around and I point at the constant beam of light that reflects towards me. We follow the direction of the light beam and come up on a solid metal hatch hidden behind rocks and bushes. "Do you think it is just a maintenance tunnel or something?" I ask him.

He shakes his head, "Do you see those two crossed hammers carved into the top here?" He points and I nod, "This is his symbol. Hephaestus is here." Zagreus grabs hold of the hatch and pulls it up slowly, his muscles tighten as he takes it in both hands and places it on the ground, the dust rises as it lands. Inside the hatch is a ladder that leads deep into the underground, I can't even see the bottom. "I'll go first."

"Are you sure?" I ask him.

"Of course, I am." Zagreus answers, he doesn't look at me. He grabs either side and begins to lower himself into the hole, catches his foot on the ladder and begins descending; once he is down far enough, I follow his lead.

As we lower ourselves down deeper, lights begin to turn on as we pass them. I hear something rumbling from above us and look up.

"Uhm... Zagreus." I stop climbing and stare at the hatch above us.

"What?" he asks, still descending the ladder.

"The hatch is closing by itself." I tell him.

"I figured it would." He continues down, unbothered by this information. I'm wondering to myself why he didn't think to mention it to me, but then I remember that he isn't talking to me right now.

When we reach the bottom of the ladder, we are in a wide, metal tunnel with lights that lead to a curve before disappearing. The sound of metal hitting metal bounces around the walls. We follow the tunnel in silence until we come around the bend and are faced with a giant workshop. There are furnaces and forges that burn so hot I feel like my eyebrows are going to burn off. We follow the metal sound and come up behind a tall man. He has gloves on, holding a hammer in one hand, and tongs that are latched to something long and metal in the other. As he hits the metal with the hammer, he turns it using the tongs. A black apron is tied around his waist, and on each leg is a support mechanism of sorts, made with gold that shines from the fires of the furnaces.

"I wondered how long it would take you to figure it out." Hephaestus speaks, his voice raw and deep. He hits the piece of metal a few more times before picking it up and sticking it into a barrel of liquid, pulling it back down and placing it on the table in front of him. He takes his gloves off, setting them on the table as well and turns to face us. "You were wondering around for a long time. I'm surprised you didn't give up."

"Not the type." Zagreus tells him.

"Well, since you made it. What do you want?" Hephaestus asks, he seems bored almost.

"What do you know of a tomb of bronze?" Zagreus asks and Hephaestus ponders for a second.

"Not practical." He finally states, "I'd choose wood personally. Of course, I'd have to be able to die for that to matter though. Hephaestus brushes past us, a slight limp in his walk and hangs his apron on a hook in the wall. "You hungry?" He asks us, beckoning us to follow him. We weave through the tools and machinery and walk through a doorway into a small apartment. The apartment walls are mostly natural rock from the mountain, but there is a large window that overlooks the countryside.

"It's beautiful." I say, making my way over to the window and looking out.

"I thought so." Hephaestus nods. "You dyin' or something?"

"Me?" I look at him confused and he nods, "No, I'm not dying."

"Why are you looking for a bronze casket then?" Hephaestus asks, he points at Zagreus, "I know it's not for this guy."

"It's for Ares." Zagreus tells him. Hephaestus doesn't react, instead he grabs a bag of chips and shoves a few into his mouth.

When he swallows, he says, "You really think he's going to fall for *that* again?" His brows raise.

"Fall for what again?" I ask him.

"It might," Hephaestus shrugs, ignoring me. "He might even do the work for you if you tell him somebody's wife is inside it."

"What are you talking about?" Zagreus asks him, Hephaestus looks surprised.

"You don't know?" He asks him, when Zagreus shakes his head, Hephaestus continues. "I'm surprised Hades didn't tell you." He sits down at the wooden dining table. "Let's see if I remember everything."

When Ares was younger, He was kidnapped by giants and held in a bronze jar, a storage jar—Hephaestus called it a storage pithos, but I had no idea what that meant so he had to clarify for me. Ares was kept in the jar for thirteen months, a lunar year, until the mother of the giants responsible for his capture, was overheard bragging about what her sons had done. Hermes with the help of Artemis, rescued Ares just before he took his last breath, and killed the two giants.

"So where is the bronze jar now?" I ask Hephaestus after he tells this tale.

"Last I heard, Aphrodite had it." He answers.

"Of course, she does." Zagreus rolls his eyes. "This whole time. This. Whole—" He punches the rock wall and the apartment shakes, "Time." He finishes.

"*Show some respect for another mans home.*" Hephaestus warns, his voice low.

"Sorry but I can't believe this." Zagreus shakes his head. "Aphrodite has had a way to take Ares down this entire time and she kept it secret from us."

"You're friends with Aphrodite?" Hephaestus asks.

"No." Zagreus and I state at the same time.

"I knew it. She has been protecting him this whole time." Zagreus scoffs.

"She might have forgotten that she had it." I try, but Hephaestus laughs at me.

"Aphrodite is a lot of things, but she isn't forgetful." He tells me.

"How do we know she didn't destroy it?" Zagreus asks.

"It was made by giants; she wouldn't be able to destroy it. Only Zeus would, and I think he liked the thought of being able to shut Ares in it when he needed, that is, until I took it from him, and Aphrodite took it from me." Hephaestus explains to us, then he turns to me. "Does that hurt?" He points to my ankle.

"Oh, no. It's fine." I tell him.

"Are you sure? I could make you a brace for it." He offers.

"Thank you but I'm fine." I assure him, he squints his eyes as he looks at my ankle, then shakes his head and looks back up at us.

"You know, if you still plan on going after Ares, I could give you a few things that might help." Hephaestus gets up, limps across the room, and rummages through a closet. He pulls out all sorts of stuff, ranging from shoes to metal armor before coming out with a golden net. "You wanna know what I did with this." The look on his face is mischievous.

"Spare us the details, I already know." Zagreus puts his hand up in protest, "But we'll take it if you're offering." Hephaestus throws the net to him; Zagreus catches it and folds it in his arms.

Hephaestus tries to give us all sorts of things from his shop. Silver bows and arrows, shields, spears, armor, and even a scepter that I have no idea what we would use for. Zagreus accepts the bow and arrows, but we leave the rest behind and make our exit. When we finally make it back to the Jeep, Andrew is sleeping peacefully in the back seat, and it is almost midnight.

On the way back home, we stop at a gas station that borders the Four-Corners for fuel and a bathroom break. I come out of the gas station and a large man stops me. He has a long beard, and even longer hair that is messy and sticks out in different directions.

"Spare any change?" He asks me, his voice is deep and I consider telling him to leave me alone, but instead I dig in my pockets, pull out a five dollar bill and hand it to the man. "Thank you, have a blessed day." He tells me, I nod and make my way back to the car. Zagreus and Andrew stop talking the second I walk up on them.

"When are you guys going to stop being mad at me?" I ask them both.

"I'm not mad, are you mad?" Andrew asks Zagreus who shakes his head.

"Oh, come on!" I groan. "I'm sorry, okay?"

"If we were mad, we'd accept your apology, but we aren't, so." Zagreus shrugs.

"I have been trapped in a car with you both for almost two weeks." I tell them, "I can tell that you're mad."

"Not mad. Just..." Andrew trails off, thinking. "*Disappointed.*" He finishes. I pout at him.

"I'm sorry." I say slower.

"Do you even know what you are apologizing for?" Zagreus asks me, crossing his arms.

I sigh, "For trying to fight Ares alone, for not paying attention and getting caught in that *stupid* bear trap and making you want my blood. For threatening to leave you if you didn't come with me. For getting us into this mess in the first place." I explain. The boys exchange a look and nod at each other.

"We accept your apology." Andrew says smugly.

"Now come here." Zagreus spreads his arms and I fall into them, Andrew hugs us from behind and the boys squeeze me so tightly I feel like I might pop.

"How hard was that?" Andrew says into my back.

"I can't breathe." I struggle and they laugh before letting me go. Andrew ruffles the hair on top of my head and we get in the car together, one last time.

When I was a kid, there was a wildfire that was burning out of control only a few miles away from my house. I remember the dark orange sky, the smell of smoke, and ash falling from the sky like snowflakes. My mom and dad scrambling around the house, deciding what was needed and what we could leave behind. They packed the cars with necessities and left the rest. Dad would water the lawn and the house along with it, he told me it might help save the house. I don't remember being afraid. It never occurred to me that we might have to leave our house behind, or that if we did, there might not be a house when we returned.

I knew there was a wildfire burning in Paradise. I saw as much on the news a week ago. But I didn't realize it was as bad as it is. I gasp audibly when we get deeper into Arizona. A thick layer of smoke covers everything like a thick blanket. Ash covers the windshield like snow. It looks like we are driving through the middle of the apocalypse. There are no cars on the road with us. Buildings look boarded up and shut down.

It occurs to me now, as I see the flames covering the mountains of my backyard that I might not have a home to return to.

9

I Am Not A Woman; I'm a God.

Even with the windows rolled all the way up and the air conditioning off, the smoke still finds its way inside of the Jeep. Andrew has his shirt pulled up to cover half of his face and I breathe through my sleeve. Paradise looks abandoned, the parking lots are empty, and the roads are devoid of any other cars. We don't stop, instead we drive straight through my tiny hometown until we pull into my driveway. My house is the only one with any lights on.

Dad and Deme are already back.

Everything looks exactly as it did when we left, only now the yard is covered in a thin layer of ash. The dark brown paint is starting to peel from the sides, the plants in the windows are still alive and vibrant. The window for my bedroom remains dark but the living room window is brightly lit behind the curtain.

I run into the house, calling for my family, and instead I find the oldest woman I have ever seen in my entire life. I cannot comprehend how old this woman looks. She has no muscles, only bones with baggy skin that hangs over them. Her eyes are hollow and dark, her hair white, and her clothes hang from her formless body.

"Hello." I blink at her.

"You must be Rose." She says, although I have no idea how she is speaking because she can't possibly be anything more than a skeleton. "My name is Avra." I continue to blink, unsure what I could possibly say to her. Footsteps approach from behind and soon Andrew and Zagreus are behind me. Zagreus doesn't miss a beat.

"You're the oracle?" Zagreus asks astonished.

"Yes, I am. It is great to see you again Zagreus." She answers him.

"Oh wow, it has been so long since I've last seen you! You haven't aged a day!" He exclaims and I look at him wide eyed. He smiles at me excitedly. "Rose, this is Avra. We go way back!" I smile to be polite but turn to Andrew and he thankfully looks as bewildered as I feel.

"How did you meet?" I force out, I notice Zagreus blush.

"Zagreus came to me in search of answers regarding his love life." She answers.

"You did?" I almost yell. I still can't believe what I am seeing. "That's...Wow." I nod awkwardly. A door closes somewhere upstairs, and I peek around the skeleton-woman to see my sister descending the stairs. When Deme sees me, she runs straight into my arms.

I hug Deme tighter and longer than I think I ever have. I breathe in the smell of her shampoo and smile.

Back when we were really young, Phoenix, Deme and I were very close. Back then being young meant that your siblings were your best friends, and we did everything together. We rode bikes and watched movies, played video games and board games, always together. But once we reached the age where our interests began to diverge, I felt alone, especially after I lost my memory. And even more so when Phoenix disappeared. It was like everyone in my tiny world was changing, growing, and becoming the people they always would be, but I was held back, the same tiny girl whose best friends were leaving her behind. Sometimes when I look at Deme, I can still see that tiny girl she used to be, who left her dolls out everywhere like they had all died in battle, the little girl who collected plastic horses and slept with every single one of her stuffed animals because she didn't want any of them to feel bad. I wonder if she feels the same way. I hug that little girl now, hoping she understands how much she means to me.

"Rose, you're hurting me." Deme says and I pull back.

"I'm sorry." I tell her, "I just missed you."

"I missed you too." She smiles.

In the living room, Dad and Deme tell us about their visit to Greece, although it feels like they are holding something back because there are times when Deme insists Dad wasn't with her and he swears he was. Avra is in the kitchen cooking something while they talk, it smells good, but I'm also not entirely convinced she can taste still. Andrew calls gabby at some point and tells her and Aphrodite to join us. We decide to eat while we wait, so we can tell them everything we have been through at the same time. Avra's skills in the kitchen are impressive, she makes us something called spanakopita that I can't get enough of. I want to kick myself for being so skeptical of her.

Instead of knocking, Aphrodite and Gabby let themselves in. Andrew holds Gabby so long I'm not sure he is ever going to let go of her and when he does, they sit so close, she might as well be sitting on his lap. I decide to exclude the intimate details of Zagreus and my relationship to the others, instead I hold his hand the entire time the three of us explain what happened on our road trip. No one was surprised that Nix decided not to come home, which makes me feel like I missed something, but I blow off the feeling. I show them the marks that are still present on my ankle from the bear trap, which makes dad angry that Nix couldn't tell Steele was a traitor. And finally, we get to our time with Hephaestus, and I can see the worry in Aphrodite's eyes growing larger.

"Aphrodite, after everything we have been through, I need you to be honest with us." I tell her delicately. We decided that, while Zagreus was allowed to be present, I would be the one to confront her about the bronze jar.

"Why wouldn't I?" She asks, rolling her eyes and twirling her hair in her fingers.

"I know you have it," I tell her, "And I need you to give me the bronze jar that imprisoned Ares." Aphrodite goes very still; I can see the gears turning in her head but before she can speak Zagreus gets in her face.

"What's your endgame?" He asks, "Were you always a traitor or did Ares get to you?"

She looks insulted, "*Traitor?* You think I'm a traitor?"

"You hid the existence of something that could help us, I mean, do you blame us?" I ask.

"No." She admits, "But I am not a traitor. I forgot I had it."

"Hephaestus said you might say that." Zagreus's brow raises.

"He could die!" Aphrodite yells, "And I love him." I sit back, not sure what to say. If I was in her position, I probably would have done the same thing. Do I really blame her for lying about it?

"Ares didn't even flinch when he burned you and the rest of Olympus to the ground, he won't hesitate to kill you this time." Zagreus tells her, "Not after all the help you've given us."

"He wouldn't." She shakes her head, "He would never hurt me like that." Zagreus looks defeated for a moment, thinking carefully about what he is going to say to her next.

"Ares killed Adonis." Zagreus's voice is low as he tries to reason with her.

"No, a boar did." She is very quiet; I can see tears building in her blue eyes.

"Ares disguised himself as a boar and pierced Adonis's heart the second you left his side, when you returned, the boar was already gone because it was Ares."

"You're lying." She sniffles.

"I was there, when Adonis entered the Underworld. He spoke of what happened to my mother as she guided him to the afterlife." Zagreus tells her. Aphrodite is very quiet, and after a moment a single tear runs down her cheek and she gets up, disappearing into the basement.

"Who is Adonis?" I ask Zagreus.

"Aphrodite's soulmate." He answers. I get up and follow Aphrodite into the basement.

The basement has been untouched since we left. Aphrodite is sitting on the couch in the middle of the room, her hands cover her face, but I can tell she is crying. I sit next to her and pull her into my arms. We don't speak as I hold her, crying in my arms but I can't help but feel jealous of how beautiful she looks even when she has tears streaming down her face and snot dripping from her nose. I reach forward, pull a tissue from the box that rests on the table in front of us and hand it to her. She takes it and blows her nose.

"Why are you so kind to me?" She asks me when she has composed herself a bit. But I don't know how to answer her.

"Why wouldn't I be?"

"Because I was nothing but cruel to you when we first met." She tells me.

"Really? I didn't notice." I smirk and she frowns, but I can see a little bit of her old self shining through.

"Honestly, tell me why." She sniffles.

"Because you deserve it." I shrug.

"I most certainly do not. I told you that you didn't have a soulmate." I can see the tears building in her eyes again.

"Yeah, you did." I nod, "But only because my soulmate wasn't interested in you."

Aphrodite shoots up straight, the tears gone from her eyes. "He told you."

"He did. But only because I asked, I think he would have taken that secret to the grave if I hadn't."

"Zagreus is immortal." She reminds me.

"You know what I mean." I roll my eyes.

"But that doesn't answer my question." She presses.

I sigh, "I guess it's because I can see you for who you really are." I start, "Aphrodite, you are the most beautiful woman I have ever seen. Your hair is never greasy, you don't get pimples, and someone could drown in your eyes. But it isn't just your looks, you are smart and calculating, cunning and ambitious. When I look at you, I see a woman who is constantly overlooked and trying to make up for it with her looks because men tell you that is all you are good for. But you are not a woman Aphrodite." She looks appalled, but I continue before she can interrupt. "You are a god."

"I am not a woman; I am a god." She repeats.

"You don't need Ares, you don't need any man, because you are powerful in your own right. You demand respect, you don't need to earn it.

"I am not a woman; I'm a god." She says again like it has become her new mantra. Aphrodite wipes her eyes, stands tall in front of me and smiles, "I am *not* a woman; I'm a *god*." When she first came to stay with us, Aphrodite changed her appearance to look younger. Now she stands taller, looking like she had when I first met her. Her features more pronounced, and less like an awkward teenager. Her long blonde hair framing her face perfectly, with an expression that could kill.

We walk back upstairs together, in her hands is not a jar, but a three-foot tall black and orange vase. On it, are drawings that could be interpreted as Ares, and I recognize some of the symbolism on it.

"That's a *jar*?" Andrew asks what I'm thinking.

"It was made by giants, technically that would be a jar to them." Gabby tells him and I can't help but laugh.

Aphrodite holds the jar out to me, "Here." she says quietly, I take it from her hands and find that it is surprisingly light-weight, I can't help but wonder if it'll be heavier when we put Ares in it. I hand the jar to Zagreus and sit back down next to him on the couch. Deme and Avra's eyes go white at the same time, I jump at this, but Zagreus holds me back.

"They're having a vision." He tells me. Both Deme and Avra come out of it at the same time and look at each other before Deme turns to me, the blood drained from her face.

"Ares knows." Deme speaks.

"What happens now?" I ask my dad who has been quiet for a long time.

"We prepare for war." He tells us.

10

In The Moonlight

I'm running. Faster and faster.

With every step, I'm gliding over the earth like I'm flying. The trees and bushes blur past me. I feel wild and more alive than I ever have before. I make my way through the woods like I had every day before this. Every inch of the forest is etched in my brain, like a map that only I can see. I turn sharply, heading towards the middle of the forest. He will be waiting there for me, in the same spot that we meet every day to play with each other.

I slow my pace down as I get closer. Something is wrong. It smells like something is burning. I stop and realize that I am surrounded by flames. The woods are burning, filling the air with smoke and ash. A man stands in front of me laughing menacingly. I inch closer to him, and he stops laughing. He pulls a spear out from behind him and the grin on his face grows wider. His eyes are dark and his hair lifts as the winds pick up around us. I am frozen in fear.

I turn and run for home; my heart beats a million beats per minute, but I realize there is nowhere for me to go. I am surrounded by the flames. I turn back and face the man. I am the protector, after all. I am supposed to keep them safe, and I cannot fail. The forest becomes unfamiliar and terrifying, but I take another step, inching closer and closer to the man until he lifts the spear, points it straight at me and with all his might, throws it at me.

I open my eyes and gasp for air.

Zagreus is next to me in an instant, a worried look on his face. I take in the rest of the room. I am in my bedroom. There is my vanity, my window, my closet with the broken folding door, I'm in my bed and Zagreus is next to me. It was a dream. It was just a dream.

Then why did it feel so real?

Zagreus looks at me. Did he ask me something? I can't remember. I don't think he did.

"It was just a dream." I insist, hoping that answers him. He seems to relax a little.

"What was the dream about?" He asks groggily.

"It was the same dream I had when my memories came back." I tell him, he rubs my back gently, "But it was different."

"How different?"

"There was fire this time." I answer, distracted as he rubs my back.

"Fire?"

"Yeah, like at the campsite. A wall of fire." I replay the dream in my mind again. It felt so real, I could smell the smoke so clearly.

"It's probably from all the smoke outside." He tells me and kisses my shoulder.

"Yeah." I agree and lay back down, "probably." Zagreus lays down next to me and closes his eyes. Soon his breathing evens out and he falls asleep, but now I am wide awake.

Maybe it wasn't a dream.

Maybe it was a vision.

The sun rises, peaking through my bedroom window and sending light and shadows across my ceiling. I look at Zagreus. His features are relaxed, he looks peaceful, happy. It is a rare way for me to see him. Without worry, or anger or even annoyance or love. There is no expression on his face for me to read and I am able to really appreciate his beauty. The way he looks like a Greek statue, or a painting. His long eyelashes, his perfect skin and chiseled jawline, the way his hair falls on his forehead. I turn back to the window, it doesn't look as smokey out, maybe they made some progress with the fires overnight. Or maybe Ares is waiting for me. Giving me a clear path to him.

"What does it feel like when you have a vision?" I ask Deme at breakfast, it seems that both of us are still early risers. I caught her off guard and mid bite of her cereal. She frowns and swallows.

"It's kind of hard to explain." She thinks on it for a minute, I sip at my coffee while I wait. "It's like someone else is taking over my body. One second, I'm me and the next, I'm someone else."

"Does it hurt?"

"Not anymore." Her nose scrunches, "But it used to. Mostly I can't even tell when it's happening." She takes another bite of her cereal; I can hear it crunch in her mouth.

"The first time I turned into a wolf, it felt like someone was snapping all of my bones." I tell her. "But now, I don't even think about it."

"I guess it's all about control with both of us then." She concludes.

"Do you ever have them when you sleep?"

"I don't think so." She answers. I don't tell her that I think I had a vision. I don't even know if I really did have one. "Are you worried about me, because I swear, I'm okay." She tells me.

"No, I was just curious." I answer her and take another sip of my coffee. She seems to accept my answer because she moves to the sink to wash her bowl without another word. I stare at the bronze jar on the counter between us, wondering how I'm going to get it out of the house.

Tonight is the full moon. I will move the jar later. Ares will have to wait one more day.

It's the least he can do.

"How does it feel to be home?" I ask her.

"It's nice to sleep in my own bed," Deme starts, "But I don't know what it is, something just feels different."

"How so?" I ask.

"Like there are two ways everything could go." She takes her empty bowl to the sink, "On one hand, you guys could catch Ares, and everything will go back to the way it was before. But on the other hand, you guys could get seriously hurt or worse and Ares could win, and nothing will ever be the same." She explains.

"I guess that makes sense, but do you really think it would be bad for everything to change?"

"Yes and no, the world is constantly changing and growing every day. But this—" She sighs deeply and rests her palms on the edge of the counter, "*This* feels final. Like I wasted all my life being one person, when in reality I'm someone completely different, and I don't have any time to really understand who this new me is before everything changes." She moves back over to me and sits down. "If you guys lose, who knows what is going to happen, I mean, what is Ares plan? Is he going to destroy the gods and the entire world with them? And if you guys win, what happens if the Gods are allowed to roam the earth again? Are they going to hurt people or are they going to fix the mess humans created and leave us be?" her questions are valid and are some of the questions I've even asked myself since I got stuck in the middle of all of this. I reach out for her hand across the table, and she takes it, giving me a light squeeze. "I'm sorry for being so crazy, it's just that ever since I got these powers, I never know what to think. These visions are so black and white, and nothing is ever just black and white, you know? They can be interpreted a million different ways, and they never show you the whole picture, just bits and pieces that you have to put together like a puzzle with no edge pieces." Deme smiles at me solemnly.

"I know your worried but try not to think about it so much. Everything will work out the way that it was meant to." I squeeze her hand, "All we can do is enjoy the ride as long as we can." I tell her.

The house begins to slowly come to life as everyone starts waking up. No one has told Gabby about the chance that Andrew could be human again, it was one of the few details left out of our retelling. After the way I had reacted to Andrew having a drop of my blood, we didn't want to break her heart if she felt one way or the other. Andrew and I are sitting on the back porch. We don't normally spend time out here, since the house is so far back from the road, my back yard is almost nonexistent. There are overgrown blackberry bushes, weeds and old toys that rot in the corner by the fence. Everyone else is inside, deciding how to go about taking Ares down, they don't know I already have a plan.

"What if I don't become human again?" Andrew asks me and I shrug.

"You'll still be my best friend." I assure him.

"But I'll eventually need human blood." He says quietly. I reach out and squeeze his arm.

"We'll figure it out. Gabby's mom works at the hospital, maybe blood bags will be enough."

"What if it isn't." He asks, "What if it has to be fresh, like Cyrus said."

"Cyrus was a lunatic." I roll my eyes thinking about him, "You won't become like him."

"But what if I do? What if I get hungry in the middle of a concert, or the mall?"

"Nobody goes to the mall anymore, so you'll be fine." I tell him, he bumps my shoulder with his.

"I mean it Rose."

"You won't." I cross my legs and face him, "Remember what Zagreus said about you becoming your best self?" I ask him and he nods. "You would never hurt someone before you turned, so wouldn't that carry over?"

Andrew sighs, "I guess. But we don't know, Cyrus could have been a monk before this or something."

"Something tells me that Cyrus was the exact same person before and after he turned." I assure him.

"I'm going to have to break up with Gabby, aren't I?" He asks.

"I don't know. I think in the end it will be her decision."

"But what if she resents me?"

"What would she resent you for?"

"I can't go to college, I can't work a day job, I probably can't have kids anymore." He goes on but the list gets more outrageous as he does.

"Stop," I tell him, "It doesn't matter, if she wants to be with you as much as you want to be with her then you will find a way to make it work." I watch as Andrew relaxes, I try to memorize his face like it is now. His brown eyes with flakes of gold, the dark freckles on even darker skin that line his cheeks. Andrew has always been my best friend, ever since kindergarten when he was being bullied on the monkey bars and I stood up for him. I am the protector; I always have been.

It feels like the longest day. Time drags on as we countdown the hours until the moon is at the highest point in the sky. We play cards, watch shows on tv, poke fun at each other for all the dumb stuff we have done, if we were to get tattoos what would we get. We do everything except talk about the inevitable, will Andrew become a human or not?

It feels weird, being here with everyone all together, laughing and joking like the world as we know it isn't doomed. More than once I catch myself staring at everyone remembering tiny details about their faces or their mannerisms. Gabby has a scar on her shoulder that I never noticed before, Deme's green eyes look almost blue in this lighting, one of Andrews locs is thicker than the rest, and Zagreus has a cowlick on the back of his head, his only flaw on his entire body. My dad smokes a cigarette on the porch with Avra, I wonder what they talk about, but I don't try to listen in.

I could smell the alcohol on my dad before he even entered the room, he has been keeping his drinking a secret for now and I'm not sure if he knows that I know but I don't say anything to him about it. He isn't getting drunk, as far as I've been able to tell, which is good enough, I guess. At least he isn't being brought home in the back of a police cruiser anymore and Deme and I are grown enough that I don't think we are in danger of becoming foster kids anymore. Maybe she will even get to graduate high school on time, unlike me, she's managed to keep up on her schoolwork during all of this. I can't even think about trying to work on math right now.

The sun goes down and the moon rises.

The time approaches and the room falls silent.

"What happens now?" Andrew asks the room, no one speaks. We sent Gabby home a few hours ago to get a change of clothes and Aphrodite went with her, now it is just my family, Zagreus, Avra, and Andrew who sit in the living room. I can tell he is nervous, but I don't say anything as he stands up with Zagreus. I'm nervous for him. Zagreus takes my hand and the three of us go outside to the front porch. It started with the three of us and we will face it the same way.

Together.

I don't know what we are waiting for, after everything we have experienced, anything could happen. The moon shines brightly above us and I wait for something, *anything* to happen.

"When I was trapped in the Underworld," Andrew speaks, breaking the silence. "I wasn't afraid of dying. I was afraid I would never see you guys again." He admits. "I figured I might see Zagreus, since he lives there, but to never see you, Rose, or my parents or—" He sighs, "*Gabby*" I look at him, there are tears in his eyes. "It was like a trial run of death, what it would feel like to never see your loved ones again. Persephone kept me in this dark room, I didn't know what day it was or how many had passed since I'd first gotten there, I had to do something to occupy my thoughts, or I felt like I would have gone insane."

"What did you do?" I ask gently, this is the first time Andrew has genuinely opened about his experience in the Underworld.

"There was a knife in the room and I—" he breathes deeply before he continues, "I used it to cut myself, and then I used my blood to write letters to you all." He rolls up his sleeve and reveals a scar shaped like a tiny crescent moon in the middle of his forearm.

"You made a sacrifice to Selene without knowing it." Zagreus says, patting Andrews back.

"When she spoke to me, I thought I was going crazy." Andrew continues, "and when she offered me an escape, I thought she meant something else."

"You thought she would kill you." I say for him, he nods.

"Anything would have been better than the loneliness I was feeling. Even that." He rolls his sleeves back down, "I never imagined I would see you guys again and when I did, it didn't matter what I had become, because I was finally *home*."

"And how do you feel now, child?" A woman's voice calls out. We all look up and a bright shapeless light is floating before us. The light slowly turns on itself, taking form until a woman stands. She has white wings that expand behind her, radiant white skin, and hair, but her lips are pink and her eyes blue. Atop her head is a golden crown that glows, illuminating the air around her head. Andrew stands in her presence; Zagreus and I follow suit. "Do you revoke the gift of a goddess?" She asks, her voice is soft and musical.

"I...I don't know." Andrew answers her and she smiles.

"I did not give you this gift to keep, sweet child." She tells him as she moves closer.

"What do you mean?" Andrew asks.

"The pain you endured was too much to ignore, I gave you the gift as a means of escape." She cups Andrew's cheek in her hand. "It was the only way Hades would let you leave with your life still intact."

"Why did you help him?" I ask her, she smiles but doesn't look away from Andrew.

"I was once very much in love, and that love was used as a toy for the gods. When I was presented with the choice of becoming the goddess of the moon, I made a vow, a sacred promise that I would never do what the others had done to me. Artemis gave me the choice and I took it so that I may spread my light on others, you too have the choice." She runs her hand down his cheek before dropping her hand at her side, "Will you remain a child of the night, or will you return to your love?" I look at Andrew, trying to figure out his answer for him, but he is very still as he contemplates her words.

"I..." He starts, unsure of himself. "I want to be human."

"And so, it shall be." She smiles proudly at him, approaches him, illuminating his face with her glow and kisses him gently on the forehead. Andrew falls to his knees and begins to cry. Selene steps back, waves goodbye and returns to a ball of light that floats up into the night sky.

I watch the ball of light until I can't see it anymore and then I go to Andrew.

"Are you...Do you feel any different?" I ask him.

"Yeah, I do." He looks up at me and smiles, "I don't feel so *hungry* anymore."

I squint at him, "That doesn't sound like you."

"Don't get me wrong, I could really go for some pizza right now." He rubs his stomach, "But just pizza, no blood or any-thing." He laughs.

I can't help myself; I hug him tightly. "I can't believe it *worked*." I cry. Zagreus pats Andrew's shoulder and I let go of him. "Let's order you some pizza, now."

Gabby shows up a little while later and when everyone is in-side getting food, I take the opportunity to sneak the jar out-side. I stash it under the front porch step and look up at the moon, whisper a thank you to Selene and go back inside.

Gabby and Andrew are inseparable. She didn't know if we were messing with her at first, since appearance wise, Andrew looks unchanged, but after a little bit of convincing and coming clean about what really happened in New Orleans with Cyrus, she finally believed us. Now, they are asleep on the couch, his arms wrapped tightly around her. As I turn out the light in the kitchen, I sneak one last look at them before heading up to my own room where Zagreus waits for me.

"Are you okay?" Zagreus asks as I shut the door behind me.

"Yeah, why?"

"I didn't know if you were still worried about whether Andrew was going to be human again or not." He explains and I relax, glad he hasn't figured out what is really bothering me.

"I mean, I was worried at first. But Selene wouldn't have shown up if she wasn't going to make him human right?"

"Probably not." He yawns and leans back in the bed. I turn the light off and climb into bed next to him, waiting for him to fall asleep. "Are you sure your dad is okay with me sleeping in here with you?" Zagreus asks after a short moment of silence.

"I don't think he is entirely for it, but he doesn't really get a say anymore." I answer.

"But it is still his house." Zagreus points out.

"Yeah," I acknowledge him, not bringing up the fact that it was me who paid the bills while he went on a drunk crusade the last few years. "It's fine though. I promise." I assure him and he seems to take my word for it because I can feel his body relax against mine.

"Are you scared?" he asks.

"Of what?"

"Of what comes next. Of whatever Ares has planned for us." Zagreus clarifies.

"I don't know if scared is the right word for it." I tell him. "But I am ready for this to be over."

"Me too." The room fills with silence and Zagreus's words hang in the air around us.

"Zagreus." I whisper.

"Yes?"

"I love you." I tell him.

"I love you too, Rose." He traces tiny circles on the lines of my palm that rests on his chest.

"Are you reading my palm or something?" I ask him quietly.

"Yes." He says.

"Okay, then tell me, what's my future?" I giggle. I swear, in the moonlight of my bedroom window, his eyes light up like a million fireflies and he smiles at me like he never has.

"Us."

Zagreus grabs me around the waist and pulls me into him. He kisses me with all of the power he possesses, making up for all the hours and minutes and seconds our lips haven't been touching. It felt like every fiber of my being was dying and he was my medicine because suddenly I feel more alive than I have in weeks. I feel stronger, happier, more passion and de-sire. Encased in blankets and sheets our bodies tangle together in a mess of wandering limbs, our lips never leaving each other. I slowly lift his shirt over his head, his eyes meet mine for a moment and I feel like I am staring into his soul. He pulls me closer and kisses me again, his hands gliding up my back, ca-ressing my skin. When my shirt falls away and my chest is ex-posed, his eyes go wide and instantly feeling insecure I attempt to cover myself, but he takes my hands in his, not letting me.

"Don't you dare." He growls in my ear. And I get goose-bumps down my neck and arms. I watch as his crystal blue eyes take me in, and it is so different from the way that anyone has ever looked at me. I feel beautiful. When his eyes make their way back up to mine, I see desire in them, but I also see the fight that is going on in his brain. He grabs the back of my neck and pulls me into him gently, our bodies fitting together perfectly, skin on skin, heartbeats syncing together. He grabs me around my waist again, his fingers tremble.

"What's wrong?" I whisper.

"I don't want to hurt you." He rests his forehead on mine, "I can't believe I'm doing this, never in my wildest dreams did I think I would be—"

"Shut up and kiss me." I tell him taking his face in my hands and pulling him into me again. In the moonlight from my window, our bodies become one, surrendering ourselves to one another.

This is the way I want to die, drowning in his love. I could catch fire and happily turn to ashes from his passion. I could die against his lips, his hips, in the emotion in his eyes as he sinks into me. Two heartbeats becoming one, indistinguishable from each other.

I don't know how long we stay like this, wrapped up in each other's arms. But soon Zagreus falls asleep, and I am listening to the way he breathes. I trace his jawline while he sleeps, a small smile gracing his lips. I could live here forever in this moment, and for a brief moment it feels like I can. Living in a world where just my touch is enough to make him smile, even in his sleep. And then the feeling subsides as I remember what comes next. The rest of the world falls asleep outside of my window and the only sound throughout the house is the sound of slumber, except for the pounding of my heart as I prepare myself for what I need to do.

11

Burn

The wind is rustling the leaves and pine needles of the trees, the birds sing a song of danger, warning me of what is waiting for me at the end of my path. My soul used to long for this place, but now it aches as the destruction of the fire becomes clear to me. I stare down at my shoes, watching as a fine layer of ash settles on them. The wind picks up again and the ash takes lift, swirling in the air around me. The fire wasn't a warning, it was a personal attack. Ares knew exactly what would hurt me the most. He started with the fires and worked his way up to my family.

My family.

They are all asleep, safe and sound in their beds. Sneaking out was never going to be the hard part of my mission, it was leaving them behind that would be hardest. But I need to do this alone.

You couldn't let them see you die.

This thought pushes me forward again. I can't begin to imagine the look on Zagreus' face as Ares kills me, I refuse to think of my sisters or even my brothers. I was never going to be able to say goodbye to them, as much as they deserved to hear me say the words, I couldn't do it. I couldn't see the fight behind their eyes as they refused to let me go.

Keep moving.

I follow the same path into the forest that I always have. I know where Ares is waiting for me. It will most likely be my final resting place if I can't figure out how the jar works. Ares proved just how ruthless he was when he got to Steele. Steele was just a puppet, a plaything to throw away when he got bored, but he did it to prove how close he could get to my family without me even blinking. He could have killed Nix, yes, but he wanted to torture me with the knowledge first. Ares probably killed Steele after he was done just because he could, and he probably told Cyrus how to find us in New Orleans, he could have even told the siren to steal Poseidon's trident.

I approach my destination. A break in the trees where an old house sits crumbling from time and the elements. The sun rises gently over the mountains, peaking through the trees that surround me. My heart beats wildly in my chest and my hands shake as I place the bronze jar on the ash covered ground in front of me.

"I'm here Ares!" I yell, a flock of birds flies overhead, "come and get me!"

He doesn't keep me waiting.

I can feel his presence before I can see him. It looms over me like a boulder has been placed on my shoulders. His footsteps rattle my bones, but I remain still as he approaches me from behind. He is not alone. There are others that walk alongside him, trying to match his stride but failing. When I turn to face him, I am not at all surprised to see who stands beside him.

"Good to see you again, love." Cyrus smirks he stands on the left side of Ares, Steele stands on his right. I ignore him and keep my eyes trained on Ares. Ares looks thrilled to see me, a devilish grin on his face.

"You aren't going to have someone else fight your battles, are you?" I ask Ares, he hardly reacts to my words. Instead, he takes a step forward and when the other two attempt to join him he waves them back.

"You don't look surprised to see my friends. Figure it all out, have you?" Ares calls to me.

"I did." I tell him.

"Don't you wanna know how I did it? Aren't you curious at all?"

"I didn't come here to talk." I answer, his grin grows wider.

"Do you really think you can take me?" He laughs, "I'm not some low-level god of chaos, dog, I'm the real deal." He states smugly. While his reference to Melinoe does surprise me, I don't react. "Wait, don't tell me you've come to sacrifice yourself?" He finally concludes and I nod, "Well this ought to be good."

"I want you to leave the world alone." I tell him. "I will let you take my life, if you spare the others and leave everyone alone."

"That's pretty vague girly, you might want to re-think your offer."

"The other gods will no longer play your games and you will not harm another soul on this planet."

"You really think I'm going to agree to that? I could kill you without blinking." Ares laughs, Cyrus and Steele mimic him. I step to the side, revealing the bronze jar behind me. Ares goes completely still—so still that I can't tell if he is breathing—his eyes darken and his smile dissipates, Cyrus keeps laughing.

"You think we're afraid of some oversized pot?" Cyrus calls out. Ares pulls a blade from his side and in one swift movement, Cyrus's head is rolling in the dirt. His body falls to the ground, dirt and ash settling into his blood as it drains from his neck. Next to him, Steele stiffens, and I can hear his heart speed up, his nervousness taking control. Ares doesn't seem to notice or care.

"Man, that guy was annoying." He chuckles but his eyes don't meet mine, he is still staring at the jar behind me. Ares is trying to cover up his fear with power, I can't fall for it but the longer he talks the more likely it is that Zagreus is going to come looking for me.

"Tell me one thing." I speak clearly, Ares raises a brow. "Why me? Why would you look the other way for everyone else but when I break the rules and tell a mortal the truth, you decide to rage out?"

"Because it was easy." He states.

Easy.

Easy?

Ares burned my forest.

Ares threatened to kill me.

And it was because it was *easy*.

I knew Ares was the god of war. The personification of brutality and bloodlust. I knew he was mocked and belittled among the other gods. But I never dreamed he would take the easy route.

I am going to make this anything *but* easy for him.

My blood boils with an intensity I have never felt before. A fire rages deep inside of me, heating every inch of my body from my toes to the top of my head, consuming me entirely. Without pause, and without a second thought, I shift into a wolf and lunge for his throat. I caught him off guard, but he still manages to throw me to the side before I can do any damage. Steele begins to shift but Ares points his dagger at him.

"Do nothing!" He tells him and Steele steps back. I recover and turn back to Ares. He squares his shoulders and prepares for a fight; I can see the rage building in his eyes, like a fire has been lit inside of him too.

Ares begins to move toward me, slow and steady, more confident of himself than I've ever been. I take a deep breath, center my point of gravity, and prepare for his attack. Ares flies across the ground, closing the space between us in seconds, barely giving me enough time to dodge to the right as he attempts to slice into me. Ash, and dirt fill the air around us, taking flight into the early morning sky. He growls and flips around to face me, I lean down, readying myself to pounce on him. Ares runs at me in full force again, but I don't back down, instead I throw myself into him, throwing him off balance and onto his back, but he manages to slice me with the dagger. I yelp and fall to his side. Ares lunges for me, reaching out to wrap his arms around my neck but I bite into his forearm and shake my head, ignoring the blood beginning to slowly drain down my side from the cut, digging my fangs deep into his muscles until I feel the muscle and sinew give way and my teeth connect to bone. Blood pours from his wounds, filling my mouth and spilling onto the ground. He drops the knife to the ground as he attempts to break free from my grasp and I manage to kick it away from us. He screams out in frustration and attempts to pull away, shaking and throwing his arms around wildly, he didn't expect me to get such a good grip on his arm. His panicked movements only cause more damage to his arm; I can feel my teeth ripping away at his skin, muscle tissue and tendons. Ares grabs the back of my neck and pulls me off his arm, my teeth rip at his skin, before he throws me. I hit a tree and fall to the ground, the wind knocked out of me. I try to compose myself, to steady my breathing but I can't and before I know what is happening, Ares' boot is colliding with my stomach and launching me again into the tree.

At first, I can't tell if the ground is shaking because I am so dazed by the damage Ares has done to me, or if he has thrown me so hard into the tree that it is falling over. But then I see it. The ground splits open next to us, a cloud of dirt and ash blinds Ares momentarily and he stumbles backwards coughing. Zagreus emerges from the hole in the ground, and it seals itself back up as he lands on his feet, facing Ares and separating us. Zagreus looks back at me, his crystal-clear blue eyes boiling over with rage. I can see the question on his face without him speaking a word. *Why?* But I don't answer, I'm so utterly shocked at his arrival that for a moment I can't process anything. Zagreus assesses my wounds and turns to Ares who at this point is covered in his own blood, his arms shredded from my teeth and spilling blood to the forest floor. Zagreus looks almost surprised that I was able to hurt Ares, but in a proud way that makes my heart flutter.

Like he is reading my thoughts, Zagreus reverts to anger, "*Rest.*" He says between his teeth and stands up to face Ares.

"Looks like someone needs to learn how to control their dog." Ares jokes.

"Shut up and pick on someone your own size." Zagreus tells him, moving closer to the god of war with purpose. Ares' eyebrows raise and he reaches for the dagger, only to find that I've kicked it farther away than he thought I had.

"Alright, show me what you got then kid." Ares tells him, I try to stand but my body is still catching up with my mind, I can't heal fast enough.

Zagreus and Ares collide together in a blur. Ares throws a punch, Zagreus ducks it and lands one on his jaw. I've never seen Zagreus fight. Even though we have been through so much together, I was always the one fighting. Even when we fought the vampires, Zagreus was alone in the hallway when the electricity exploded, I never got to see what he could do until now. He starts with defense; I can see him calculating every move that Ares is about to make and deflecting it with little effort. But as the fight carries on the impulse to finish the fight overtakes Ares and his moves become less planned out.

Ares grabs Zagreus and throws him at a tree but Zagreus somehow corrects the force of the throw and lands a few feet in front of me unharmed, his feet sliding across the dirt and ash, sending it into the air. I can't tell what Zagreus is trying to do, but so far it looks like he is just tiring Ares out. Ares whistles ear-piercingly loud and Steele reacts to it by pinpointing my location and running towards me. Zagreus tries to stand in the middle of us, but I growl at him and slide through his legs, re-acting faster than my body can think I lunge for Steele before he can hurt Zagreus. Since Steele is so top heavy, I aim for his ankles, even with his half human body, Steele shouldn't be able to grab at me fast enough. I bite down firmly on his heel, my teeth scraping against his bones, and he falls. Zagreus, now con-fident I can handle myself against Steele, turns back to Ares.

I can't keep track of both Ares and Steele, so I focus solely on taking down Steele. He howls in pain, reaching for his ankle to rip me off him but I move before he can grab me. The only other wolf I've ever fought was Nix and even then, I wasn't try-ing to hurt him. Steele is twice the size Nix is and has a clear-cut advantage, but his overconfidence could be a disadvantage, and I've been a wolf longer than him.

I know that I have already rebroken some ribs from being thrown to the ground, the cut on my side from the dagger heal-ing—but not healed enough, and my left paw hurts where my wrist would be. Probably sprained, but dodging the attacks is much more difficult now. Steele reaches for me again, and I attempt to slide under him, but he catches me mid-air and throws me down to the ground hard enough that I let out a sharp whimper. Steele is standing over me, getting ready for the final blow. The one that will kill me. With one swift move-ment, he lunges for me, and I roll to the side avoiding his claws. I stand and compose myself as he trips over himself. I use his stumble to my advantage and attack his side, planting my teeth firmly into his side and puncturing his skin. He howls with pain again and tries to grab me, but his reach is too much, and he can't get a grasp on me. I bite harder and he falls to the ground, I feel his body shift back into a human and I let go.

I never wanted to kill him, I only wanted to keep him from fighting. I figure that in the end, Ares was merely weaving lies into Steeles head. Lily had told me that he was still young, still learning how to control himself. Ares was grooming Steele the entire time, somehow knowing I would find my brother before I'd even considered it. Ares was two steps ahead of us the entire time, until I managed to surprise him by turning myself in. Steele shouldn't be punished for that, and as I watch his eyelids drift closed, he barely fights unconsciousness.

I focus on Ares and Zagreus just as Ares throws him like a spear into the middle of a tree trunk. Zagreus lands on the ground and doesn't get up. I want to run to him but if I do there is no chance that Ares doesn't grab me and rip me in half. Ares claps his hands together and out of thin air a spear appears in his hands. Like Poseidon's trident, Ares spear is massive, with a thick wooden handle and a golden spearhead. The clouds darken above us, and each step that Ares takes towards me is like thunder. The anger in his eyes burns with a rage I have never seen before, like his eyes are made of flame. The forest becomes unfamiliar in the darkness that grows around us. I knew this was coming, I knew that Ares was going to be too much for us to take down.

I take a step forward.

I have already seen this in my dreams. I knew this was coming, it was just a matter of time. I am the protector and maybe, just maybe, Ares will show mercy to the others if I let him kill me. Ares lifts the spear, points it straight at me and with all his might, throws it at me. I brace for the inevitable impact, closing my eyes, standing still, and welcoming the death that was shown to me.

"NO!" A familiar voice echoes around me.

I have just enough time to open my eyes before the spear enters my sister's body.

The world moves in slow motion around me. I return to my human state, Zagreus wakes up, Dad is yelling something as Aphrodite holds him back. It all blurs together as I lose my focus, crawling to my sister. Deme has rolled to her side, her body curled around the spear. Her precious blood *pooling* into the earth under her. The spearhead is buried up to the shaft in the middle of her chest. I have to *do* something, *try* anything to stop this. I pull her head into my lap, moving the strands of hair from her face. "It's okay," My voice sounds foreign to me as I speak, "You're going to be okay." I lie. My hand—my whole body is shaking.

Deme is dying.

My little sister is dying in my arms.

Her hand reaches out and I clutch it tightly, ignoring her blood now covering my own hand.

In this moment it is just the two of us. Deme and me. Little sister and big sister. The protector and the protected.

It was supposed to be me.

Deme's eyes have closed, but her chest moves slowly up and down. Tears slide down my cheeks and I hold my breath. Everything is still. The world is quiet around us. All I can do is watch as my sister takes her final breath and her grip on mine loosens. For a moment, I sit there, watching my tears fall onto her still face.

All I ever wanted was to keep her safe. I failed.

My sister is dead.

My sister is dead.

My sister is *dead*, and Ares is laughing.

I lay her head back gently on the ground and release her hand.

I want to kill someone, I want to scream, and I want to run as far away as I possibly can because my sister is dead. She is gone and she is never coming back. The little girl who I watched grow up, who I took care of, who was the only person who truly knew me, is now gone.

Darkness swallows me. I can't see or breathe or feel anything.

I close my eyes tightly.

And when I opened them again, all I could see was red.

Red from the blood now cooling on the ground beneath my sister, on my hands.

Red from the fires that burned through the forest.

Red from the anger, *raging* through my veins.

I stand next to my sister's body and turn to face the man who killed her. I take one step, then another towards him. His laugh echoes through the burned trees around me. I am going to kill him. My scream sounds more like a war-cry as a run towards him. Ares grips his knife tightly, preparing for my attack as he laughs.

The sky cracks in a bright white light, stopping me on my heels. A thunderous voice screams from the sky. I take a step backwards, shielding my eyes from the light.

"Enough!" the voice calls out. Lighting strikes the ground between Ares and me three times, and as the electricity subsides three men are standing where it struck. The man in the middle is the tallest, with a long beard and hair that curls around his face. The other two men, I recognize, one is Poseidon, standing tall and proud with his trident, the last man I only recognize because he looks so similar to Zagreus, with his dark hair and piercing blue eyes, he carries a helmet in his hands that looks like a skull with a crown of daggers, this must be Hades. Ares stops laughing as he looks at the men standing before us. Zagreus slowly gets up and makes his way to my side, taking my hand in his. I don't understand why no one is moving until Ares speaks.

"Father." He breathes, the man blocking my way to Ares must be Zeus.

"Ares, what have you done?" the man speaks, his voice steady, showing no emotion.

"I was taking care of business." Ares tells him through gritted teeth.

"Nonsense." Zeus holds up his hand, "Do not stand beside me and spin your tales, you double-faced liar. Wars and battles, forever quarreling with those who do not deserve it." Ares looks uncomfortable as his father speaks to him. I focus on Zeus's face, something about him seems familiar. "I have humored your silly games long enough. Stand down, my son."

Ares doesn't move, "Do you really want to do this again old man." He spits.

"Ares, you are my child, but you are insufferable, and I will not stand for this behavior any longer." Zeus tells him, "Stand down."

"And if I don't?" Ares growls, but Zeus doesn't even flinch. Instead, the king of the gods holds his arm out, his hand extended outwards. The bronze jar that I'd forgotten about flies into his hand.

"Ares, for killing an oracle and attempting to bring down your brethren, I command you to stand down or face your prison." Zeus speaks with a finality in his tone. Ares blinks at him for a moment before lifting his dagger once more.

"Make me." Ares spits, but before he can even think about using the blade, Zeus removes the lid of the pithos, and it sucks Ares inside. Zeus closes the lid, snaps his fingers and in a flash of lightning the jar is gone from his hands. Zeus turns to Zagreus and me and I immediately realize where I know him from.

"I know you." I tell him and Zeus smiles at me, "I gave you money at that gas station."

"You proved yourself worthy." He tells me before he frowns, "I apologize on behalf of my son. Your loss is felt among the gods." I swallow back my tears.

"What happens now?" I ask him.

"The world will return to the way it was always meant to." He tells me, "Without the threat of Ares looming over their heads, the gods will return to power."

"Father," Zagreus says, I look at him confused but he continues, "Does this mean what I think it does."

"It does." Zeus nods, "The gods will be allowed to interfere in mortal lives again. If they should see fit to." He looks around at the destruction Ares caused and his eyes land on my sister's body. "Such a waste of a beautiful life. I will place a memorial of her sacrifice among the stars, but first I must attend to a prisoner." Before he leaves, Zeus places his hand over my sister's body and a single yellow flower grows and blooms from the blood-soaked and ash covered ground.

"Should've used the shell." Poseidon pokes lightly at my ribs with the end of his trident that isn't pointy, and I wince, "Been too long since my last battle." I'm reminded of the siren once more and I shiver at the thought of what he could do in an actual fight. Poseidon nods at both me and Zagreus before he follows Zeus back to the center of the clearing. Hades approaches me next and holds out his hand, I take it, and he lifts my hand to his lips and kisses the top of my hand.

"I wish we were meeting under different circumstances." Hades tells me, his voice is smooth like honey, with a deep controlled tone, much like Zagreus. Hades nods at his son next to me, "You have chosen well." He smirks and Zagreus' cheeks burn red. Hades turns back to me, "I will ensure your sister is well taken care of." He tells me solemnly, but I can't speak so I muster a smile and nod. Hades drops my hand and stands with his brothers before the three of them disappear with another lightning strike.

12

The End

There are moments that are so engrained into my brain, that it feels like I am still there. I remember falling to my knees as my father rushed to the lifeless body of my sister. I remember the sound of his voice as he screamed out—hoarse and raw as he clung to her body, willing her to just open her eyes.

Just open your eyes.

I don't remember going home. I don't remember falling asleep. I don't remember when Phoenix came home.

There are more details. Like how Gabby came by every day and crawled in bed beside me, wrapping her arms around me, holding me while I tried to fall asleep. The brightness of the sky outside, sunlight filtered through the curtains of my bedroom window. Zagreus kissing my forehead as he checks on me in the middle of the night, the way he never left my side, not even for a minute.

In time, they all tell me.

In time I will feel better.

Not only had my sister died, but a part of me died with her. Stories about us could no longer be told from both of our perspectives. And I will think of her during every important moment of my life. Memories could be told but not shared.

I couldn't save her.

And the guilt of not saving her will eat away at my bones, picking at them bit by bit, piece by piece like a vulture, until there is nothing left.

The house is quiet, empty, filled with shadows. I don't know how many days have passed or how many hours I have slept. I shower, I dress, I eat.

I only briefly stare at the door across the hall, never daring to enter the room, *her room* again.

I do not cry at her funeral. I do not give a speech. I do not look at the large photo of my smiling sister in the middle of the cemetery. I do not look at her friends in the crowd, or her ex-boyfriend as he sobs behind us. Instead, I listen to the birds as they sing in the trees around us. Deme loved birds, although I hadn't remembered until this moment. Mom got her a book all about birds when she was a child, I can still see her tiny fingers as they flipped through the pages, the smile of absolute joy on her face. A robin lands on the ground in front of me, I recognize it from the book. It has a large, round body and long legs, its belly is a reddish-orange color. The robin bounces around on the dirt, looks at me for a moment and flies away.

I sit on a concrete bench that looks out onto a man-made lake. I sat in this spot during my mother's funeral, only this time it is Zagreus that comes to get me instead of my father.

He sits beside me without words, folds his hands in his lap and joins me in this moment.

"I want to see her." My voice comes out unfamiliar, these are the first words I have spoken in I don't know how long. Zagreus sighs.

"She needs time." He tells me, "To adjust to the Underworld."

To adjust to being dead. I want to say, instead I tell him, "Soon." He doesn't respond, instead he nods his head gently and takes my hands into his. Together we sit in front of the lake until the sun sets and the crowd disperses, until we are the only ones left in the cemetery.

January folds into February and then March, somehow without me even noticing. The days grow longer and warmer. I return to school, I study, I come home. Zagreus comes and goes, I don't know what he does when he is gone, I don't ask either. Sometimes he comes back smelling like paint or has wood chips in his hair. We watch movies together at night, I show him the video games I used to play with my siblings, we talk about current events, and we sleep in each other's arms.

Deme's absence was a solid thing, a burden that I carry in addition to my grief, yet I know that I will continue to live. Sometimes that knowledge seemed like the worst part. The spaces between missing her grow longer, then when I do remember, it is with a stabbing pain to my heart, and I feel guilt.

Guilt because it has been too long.

Guilt, because it should have been me.

Andrew, Gabby, and I graduate together. We celebrate with our classmates, throw our caps into the air as a symbol of our freedom. I hug my father who reeks of alcohol and cigarettes. I take the flowers Zagreus has picked out for me. I smile for the pictures when I'm asked to.

My classmates all move on, they go to college, get married.

I stay in Paradise, wishing I could be like them.

The world didn't change much after Zeus allowed the Gods back into mortals' lives. At first, it didn't seem like things would ever change, but eventually there were small changes. The Flowers in spring bloomed bigger and more colorful than they ever had. News stations all over the country were reporting that crops had doubled since the year before, they reported that it was due to the soil levels being better, but Zagreus told me that Demeter had taken her rightful place in the world of agriculture and was ensuring the harvests would be the best we'd seen in centuries. Couples who had trouble conceiving were now expecting thanks to Hera's presence. Sickness was at an all-time low along with hunger. More trees are growing, and the bees are thriving.

The world was finally healing.

Aphrodite didn't stick around after Ares was captured. It was months before we got word that she was back in town. She was opening a therapy center that focused on people who had been abused in relationships. When I see her in passing, neither of us make the step to speak to each other, instead she looks at me with understanding and nods in my direction. Maybe someday I will have the courage to enter her facility, to face everything that I have gone through, but for now I only nod back at her, the same understanding in my eyes.

The oracle of Delphi, Avra—who had taught my sister to control her visions—confirmed to me a few weeks after her death, that what I had seen all those weeks ago, was a vision. That for some strange reason, I had also received the oracle gift from my mother. I would continue to live, to slowly age for the rest of time, a gift or punishment I didn't know.

Zagreus walks with me in the forest. I haven't been here in months, not sure if I am ready. But Zagreus takes his time with me. He holds my hand and stops when I need to take a breath. The forest has begun to heal from the fires. New plants sprout under the dried pine-needles. Flowers bloom in the ashes, birds sing, squirrels run up trees. The planet can heal, no matter how bad the scar. Nature will always find a way.

The universe always finds a way. Hecate's words ring in my ears as if it were yesterday.

Zagreus makes me wear a blindfold the closer we get to his destination, but I know where he is taking me. I know these woods like the back of my hand, like an invisible map that only I can see. When he removes the blindfold, I am standing in a place that is familiar, but it is not at the same time.

We used to come here as kids. I don't know who found it first, maybe it was me, maybe Andrew or Zagreus, but the old run-down house in the middle of the woods was ours. Our home away from home. Now it is not run-down, it is beautiful. The one-story home that stands before me is almost unrecognizable. It has a low-pitched gable roof, a small, covered porch covered in planters filled with flowers, a flagstone walkway leading up to it. The walls are painted yellow, the front door is red. Growing in pots and all around are the same yellow flower that Zeus had grown from the blood of my sister.

"You did this." I whisper.

"I did this for *you*." Zagreus grips my hand and I squeeze it.

"No, this place was never mine." I turn to face him, "It was *ours*."

I kiss him like I have never kissed him before. Until I don't know if it has been minutes, hours, or days. It was blissful oblivion, not like the ones we shared before, hungry, desperate, and wanting. This kiss was soft, so careful on my lips that it was like someone was running their fingers along them. So careful it was quiet, not a shout, like a whisper saying, "I love you."

Zagreus pulls away and rests his forehead against mine, "If I kiss you all day, every day of my life, for the rest of our lives, it still won't be enough." He whispers.

Two Years Later

I knew what I was walking into before I even got out of the
car.

Aside from the dried-out weeds that wrap around the rail-
ings and the sun-dried paint chips that line the walls, the house
looks relatively unchanged from the last time I was here.

I sit in my car an extra minute, just to take it all in. The
memories of my life, living inside of these walls. If only they
could talk.

I walk up the rickety steps and reach for the front door. I
knock a bottle over as I open the door, the sound of it rolling
along the floor rings through the house, bouncing off the walls
and up into the air around me. I follow the trail of bottles to
the living room.

A single beer bottle rests on its side on the table next to
my father's chair. I round the table to face him, reaching out to
him.

Cold to the touch.

Not breathing.

No pulse.

I sit on the front step waiting, for the sheriffs, and the am-
bulance that will take him away. The image of him still very
clear in my mind. I hold his letter in my hands, his writing so
similar to my own.

My father could recover from the loss of his wife.

He would *never* recover from the loss of his child.

I bury him in the plot between my mother and sister, Nix does not attend this funeral. Not that I blame him for his absence, they never got along, and dad was less than a father figure to him. But it would have been nice to see him, nice to not have to carry this burden alone.

I didn't know it at the time, but I would never see my brother again. He married Lily, they have a child of their own now. They send me Christmas cards in the mail, and I display them on the stone fireplace Zagreus built for me.

Andrew and Gabby eloped in Vegas after graduation and Gabby is currently expecting. Andrew still calls me every night and I listen to his excitement for the new baby, Andrew's mother insists they move back to Paradise, but they are still deciding.

The sun rises and the sun sets. Life continues. The universe always finds a way.

My life would continue, even if my sisters and my fathers didn't.

After all, death is not the end.

Especially when you are married to his son.

Acknowledgements

To be honest, writing these acknowledgments is difficult because I don't really know where to start. I started writing In The Shadows over ten years ago, when I was still in high school just looking for a way to escape. Back then, I'd never imagined how much this story about Greek Gods and werewolves would mean to me, how much it would mean to other people.

Firstly, I would like to thank every single person who picked up one of my books and gave it a chance, I would never have made it to this point without you and your support. It truly means the world to me.

My sister, who spent countless hours helping me edit, brainstorm ideas, and listening to my crazy ideas, deserves more recognition than anyone. You have been my rock through-out this entire trilogy and will most likely continue to be my rock for any other stories I feel inclined to write in the future. You let me model Rose's character after your dear Rosie, and through these novels, she will continue to live on for years and years.

My brother, who continues to inspire my creativity on a day-to-day basis. You have supported me for my entire life, whether it was from my side or the other side of the world. You have never questioned who I am, and always understood the darkness that lives in our hearts can be used for goodness. You once told me that growing up was over-rated and not to listen when others said I should, and I will always strive to remember this and live each day without caring what anyone thinks about me.

Mom, mine was the first book you read in years and you were so patient when I refused to give you any spoilers or tell you anything about what happens. You finally have the whole story. You have done nothing but shout from the rooftops to anyone who would listen about my book. Without a doubt, you are my number one fan.

Chase, my heart has been yours from the moment I met you. The way our lives were woven together, it is hard to believe it wasn't fate. I am incredibly lucky to have you by my side, fighting my battles when I need you, standing by my side when I don't, and bringing me back to earth when my thoughts start to overpower my heart. Thank you for proving that true love exists. You are the Riker to my Troi, the Tuxedo Mask to my Sailor Moon, the Nick Miller to my Jessica Day, the Major Lilywhite to my Olivia Moore: I could do this all day, but I'm sure you get the picture. It is you and only you, for the rest of my life.

Taylor, our friendship is the definition of epic—almost like it was written in the legends itself. We have been through so much and you have never left my side. From the very beginning, whether it was taking author photos in the forest or prom night at the park, I can always count on you to have my back. Our friendship will be a story that can stand on its own. Thank you for your unwavering support.

To my co-workers who became my friends, Bailey, Hailey, and Brittney, you three are the true definition of a ride or die. You all love so fiercely and I am so grateful to have you in my life. I cannot wait for you to become everything you have ever dreamed, because you deserve it; each one of you. I hope someday soon you three will be joining me at the author conventions and book festivals at tables of your own.

Angie, Emmalee, Tara, Chris, Keith, Dustin, literally ever single member of my Sawmill family, I will forever cherish you. You all treat me like I'm a part of your own families. You bought my books, my art, shared all of my posts and have genuinely never let me down. I hope I can and do the same for you all.

To every member of my family, blood related or not, I cannot thank you all enough for joining me on this crazy rollercoaster. It would take me pages and pages to thank you all individually, but even if your name isn't on these pages, I hope you know that you all mean the world to me.

To the readers who have visited me in person at conventions or festivals, or bought my books online, thank you too. I would have given up on these books without you and your support. Meeting you guys has been a highlight of my career, and of my life. Thank you.

And lastly, thank you to the incredible artists who have unknowingly created the soundtrack to my books. I hope someday these books land on your laps and they inspire you just as your music has done for me.

Randee Lee, professionally known as R.L. Nelson, has been writing stories as long as she could hold a pencil. What started as a childhood passion for story-telling, has become her lifelong passion. There is nothing Randee enjoys more than writing (and reading) stories that are heart-wrenching, with some humor and a hint of romance. When she's not dreaming up new stories to tell, you can find Randee spending her time with family, playing video games, and painting, or binge-watching true crime dramas.

For more information visit her website www.AuthorRLnelson.com